They climbed the hill to the house.

Halfway up the slope, Mattie stumbled against some unseen obstruction and clutched Ethan's sleeve to steady herself. A wave of warmth went through him. For the first time he stole his arm around her. She didn't resist. They walked on as if they were floating on a summer stream.

A Background Note about *Ethan Frome*

Ethan Frome takes place in rural Massachusetts at the turn of the twentieth century. People in the village of Starkfield and on neighboring farms pick up their mail at the post office. They get around by walking or by driving horse-drawn vehicles. The nearest public transportation—the train—is miles from the village. Starkfield and nearby farms are lit by candlelight and gaslight, not electricity. They're heated by fireplaces and wood- and coal-burning stoves. In and around Starkfield, the industrial age hasn't yet arrived.

EDITH WHARTON

ETHAN FROME

Edited, and with an Afterword,
by Joan Dunayer

ETHAN FROME

TP THE TOWNSEND LIBRARY

For more titles in the Townsend Library,
visit our website: **www.townsendpress.com**

Townsend Press, Inc.
1038 Industrial Drive
West Berlin, New Jersey 08091

ISBN 1-59194-047-8

Library of Congress Control Number:
2005922985

CONTENTS

CHAPTER I

I heard the story, bit by bit, from various people, and, as generally happens in such cases, the story was different each time.

If you know Starkfield, Massachusetts, you know the post office. If you know the post office, you must have seen Ethan Frome drive up to it; drop the reins on his hollow-backed, reddish-brown horse, Bay; and drag himself across the brick pavement to the white colonnade. And you must have asked who he was.

It was at the post office that I saw Ethan for the first time, several years ago. The sight pulled me up sharp. Although he was only the ruin of a man, he was the most striking figure in Starkfield. It wasn't so much his great height that distinguished him (Starkfield residents tend to be tall). It was his careless, powerful look, despite a lameness that checked each of his steps like the jerk of a chain. There was something bleak and unapproachable in his face. He was so stiff and grizzled that I took him for an old man and was surprised to hear that he wasn't much older than fifty. I learned this from Harmon Gow, who had driven the stagecoach from Bettsbridge to Starkfield in pre-trolley days and knew the history of every family on his route.

"He's looked that way ever since he had his smash-up, and that will be twenty-four years ago come next February," Harmon said between reminiscent pauses.

I gathered from Harmon that the "smash-up" had drawn the red gash across Ethan's forehead and so shortened and warped his right side that it cost him a visible effort to take the few steps from his buggy to the post office window.

Ethan would drive in from his farm every day around noon. Because that was when I fetched my mail, I often passed him on the post office porch or stood beside him while we waited for the postmaster to finish handing out the mail. Ethan would come punctually, but he seldom received anything other than a copy of the *Bettsbridge Eagle*, which he would put, without a glance, into his sagging pocket. Every so often, the postmaster would hand him an envelope addressed to Zenobia, or Zeena, Frome. Usually the address of some medicine manufacturer appeared in the envelope's upper left corner. Ethan would pocket these envelopes, too, without a glance, then turn away with a silent nod to the postmaster.

Everyone in Starkfield knew Ethan and gave him a greeting suited to his grave manner. His habit of not speaking was respected. It was only rarely that one of Starkfield's older men detained him for a word. When this happened, Ethan would listen quietly, his blue eyes on the speaker's face, and answer so softly that I never heard his words. Then he would climb stiffly into his buggy, gather up the reins in his left hand, and drive slowly away toward his farm.

"Was it a bad smash-up?" I asked Harmon, looking after Ethan's retreating figure and thinking how handsome he must have been before his strong shoulders were bent out of shape and his thick blond hair started to gray.

"Worst kind," Harmon said. "More than enough to kill most men. But the Fromes are tough. Ethan probably will live to a hundred."

At the moment Ethan, having climbed to his seat, was leaning over to check that a wooden box he'd placed in the back of the buggy was secure. The box had a druggist's label on it. I saw his face as it probably looked when he thought he was alone. "That man live to a hundred?" I exclaimed. "He already looks dead and in hell!"

Harmon drew a slab of tobacco from his pocket, cut off a wedge, and pressed it into his leathery cheek. "I guess he's been in Starkfield too many winters. Most of the smart ones get away."

"Why didn't *he*?"

"Someone had to stay and care for his folks—first his father, then his mother, then his wife. There never was anyone but Ethan.

"And then the smash-up?"

Harmon chuckled sardonically. "That's right. Then he had to stay."

"I see. Others have taken care of him since then?"

Harmon passed his tobacco to the other cheek. "No. Ethan always has been the one to take care of others."

Harmon conveyed the story as much as his mental and moral reach permitted. There were gaps, and I sensed that the story's deeper meaning lay in these gaps. One comment especially stuck in my mind: "I guess he's been in Starkfield too many winters."

Before my own time in Starkfield ended, I learned what that meant. I had come in the era of trolleys, bicycles, and rural delivery. Communication was easy between the scattered mountain villages. The valleys' bigger towns, such as Bettsbridge and Shadd's Falls, had libraries, theaters, and YMCAs, where young people could go for recreation. But when winter descended on Starkfield and the village lay under a sheet of snow perpetually renewed from the pale skies, I began to see what life there must have been during Ethan's young manhood.

My employers had sent me on an engineering job connected with construction of an electricity powerhouse at Corbury Junction. A carpenters' strike had delayed the work for such a long time that I had found myself anchored at Starkfield, the nearest habitable spot, most of the winter. At first I had chafed. Gradually, under the hypnotizing effect of routine, I had begun to find a grim satisfaction in the life.

During the early part of my stay, I'd been struck by the contrast between the climate's vitality and the community's deadness. Day by day, after the December snows ended, a blazing blue sky had poured down light on the white landscape, which had glittered. You would think that such an atmosphere would enliven people, but it seemed to produce no change except to further slow Starkfield's sluggish pulse. This phase of crystal clearness was followed by long stretches of sunless cold, when I felt the force of Harmon's remark, "Most of the smart ones get away." I wondered what obstacles had hindered Ethan's flight.

During my stay at Starkfield, I lodged with Ruth Hale, a middle-aged widow. Her father, Jim Varnum, had been Starkfield's lawyer. The Varnum house, where Ruth and her mother Nancy lived, was Starkfield's mansion. It stood at one end of Main Street. Its classic portico and small-paned windows looked down a path between Norway spruces to the slim white steeple of the Congregational church. The Varnum fortunes were in decline, but Ruth and Nancy did what they could to preserve their dignity. In particular, Ruth had a wan refinement in keeping with her pale, old-fashioned house.

Every evening, in a parlor with mahogany furniture, I listened to a history of Starkfield. More refined and educated than her neighbors, Ruth judged them with detachment. I hoped to learn the missing facts of Ethan's story from her, or at least the key to his character. Her mind was a storehouse of anecdotes. Any question about her acquaintances brought forth a volume of detail. But she was reluctant to speak of Ethan or his affairs. No matter how persistently I sought information, she would say little more than "Yes, I knew them both. It was awful." The subject clearly distressed her.

When I asked Harmon why Ruth was so reluctant to speak on the subject, he said, "She's always been as nervous as a rat. She was the first one to see them after they were picked up. It happened right below the Varnums' house, at the bend of the Corbury road, about the time that Ruth got engaged to Ned Hale. The young people all were friends. I guess Ruth can't bear to talk about it. She's had troubles enough of her own."

No one in Starkfield would explain the devastated look of Ethan's face. I might have contented myself with the patchy story I pieced together if it hadn't been for Ruth's silence and, a short time later, personal contact with Ethan.

Each day, someone from Michael Eady's stables would drive me from Starkfield to

Corbury Flats, where I would catch a train for Corbury Junction. But in mid-winter Michael's horses fell ill. The illness spread to Starkfield's other stables. For two days I was unable to get to the train station. Then Harmon mentioned that Ethan's horses were healthy and Ethan might be glad to drive me.

I stared. "Ethan? I've never even spoken to him. Why would he put himself out for me?"

"I didn't say he'd put himself out. He'd be glad to earn a dollar," Harmon responded.

I'd heard that Ethan was poor and that the sawmill and his farm's dry acres yielded scarcely enough to sustain his household through the winter. Still, I was surprised.

Harmon continued, "When a man's been sitting around like a hulk for more than twenty years, seeing things that need doing, it eats into him, and he loses his grit. That Frome farm was always about as bare as a milk pan after the cat's been around, and that old mill is nearly worthless. When Ethan could sweat over both of them from sunrise to sunset, he squeezed a living out of them. But even then his folks ate up almost everything. I don't see how he gets by. First his father was kicked in the head by a horse and went softheaded;

before he died, he gave away money as freely as quotes from the Bible. Then his mother got so senile and arthritic that she dragged along for years as weak as a baby. Ethan's wife, Zeena, needed more doctoring than anyone else in the county. Sickness and trouble— that's what Ethan's had on his plate ever since the first helping."

The next morning when I looked out, I saw Bay between the Varnum spruces. Throwing back his worn bearskin, Ethan made room for me in the sleigh at his side. After that, he drove me to the train station every morning for a week. Every afternoon he drove me back to Starkfield, through the icy night. The distance each way was barely three miles, but Bay's pace was slow. Even with firm snow under the runners, the trip took us nearly an hour.

Ethan drove in silence, the reins held loosely in his left hand. Against the white background of snow, under his helmet-like cap, his seamed face looked like that of an ancient hero. He never turned his face to mine or responded to my chitchat or questions with more than monosyllables. He seemed part of the mute, melancholy landscape, an incarnation of frozen woe. There was nothing unfriendly in his silence. I sensed that his feelings simply were bound below the surface; he lived too deeply isolated for casual access. I sensed that his loneliness was partly the result of personal tragedy, party the result of many Starkfield winters.

Only twice the distance between us was momentarily bridged, increasing my desire to know more. Once, I mentioned an engineering job I'd been on the previous year in Florida. I commented on the contrast between the winter landscape around us and Florida's climate. To my surprise, Ethan suddenly said, "I was down there once. For a long time afterward, I could imagine the sight of it in winter. But now the memory is all snowed under." He didn't say anything else.

Another day, on the train, I found that I was missing a volume of *Popular Science* that I had carried with me to read. I didn't think about the book anymore until I got into the sleigh that evening and saw it in Ethan's hands.

"I found it after you were gone," he said.

I put the book into my pocket, and we dropped back into our usual silence. As we crawled up the long hill from Corbury Flats to the Starkfield ridge, I became aware in the dusk that Ethan had turned his face to mine.

"There are things in that book that I didn't know the first thing about," he said. His voice had a note of resentment. He was evidently surprised and slightly aggrieved at his own ignorance.

"Does that sort of thing interest you?" I asked.

"It used to."

"There are one or two rather new things in the book. There have been some strides lately in biochemistry." For a moment I waited for a response that didn't come. Then I said, "If you'd like to look through the book, I'll be glad to leave it with you."

He hesitated. "Thank you. I'll take it."

Ethan was so straightforward that I was sure his curiosity about the book was based on genuine interest in its subject. The contrast between his outer situation and his inner needs was poignant. I hoped that this chance for him to satisfy some of those inner needs might make him more communicative. But something in his past or present apparently had driven him too deeply into himself for any casual impulse to draw him out.

At our next meeting Ethan didn't refer to the book. Our conversation seemed fated to remain as one-sided as before.

Ethan had been driving me to the train station for about a week when one morning I looked out of my window into a thick snowfall. The height of the white waves massed against the garden fence and along the church's wall showed that the storm must have continued all night. The drifts were likely to be heavy in the open. I thought it probable that my train would be delayed, but I had to be at the powerhouse for an hour or two that afternoon. I decided that, if Ethan showed up, I'd push through to the train station and wait there until my train came. Actually, I never doubted that Ethan would come. He wasn't the kind of man to let a snowfall interfere with his business. At the appointed hour his sleigh glided up through the snow.

I was getting to know him too well to express either wonder or gratitude at his keeping his appointment. But I exclaimed in surprise as I saw him turn Bay in a direction opposite to that of the Corbury road.

"The railroad's blocked by a freight train that got stuck in a drift below the Flats," Ethan explained as we headed off into the stinging whiteness.

"Where are you taking me, then?"

"Straight to Corbury Junction, by the

shortest way," he answered, pointing up School House Hill with his whip.

"To the Junction? In this storm? It's a good ten miles!"

"Bay will do it if you give him time. You said you had some business there this afternoon. I'll get you there."

He said it so quietly that I could only answer, "You're doing me a great favor."

"That's all right."

Abreast of the schoolhouse the road forked. We dipped down a lane to the left, between hemlock boughs bent by the snow's weight. I often had walked that way on Sundays. I knew that the solitary roof showing through bare branches near the bottom of the hill was that of Ethan's sawmill. The mill's idle wheel loomed above a stream with yellow-white spume. A cluster of sheds sagged under their load of snow. As we drove by, Ethan didn't even turn his head.

About a mile farther, on a road I never had traveled, we came to an orchard of starved apple trees among slate outcroppings that nuzzled up through the snow like animals pushing out their noses to breathe. Beyond the orchard lay two fields, their boundaries lost under drifts. Above the fields, huddled against the white immensities of land and sky, was one of those lonely New England farmhouses that make the landscape even lonelier.

"That's my place," Ethan said with a sideway jerk of his lame elbow.

The scene was so depressing that I didn't know what to say. The snow had ceased. A flash of sunlight exposed the house on the slope above us in all its plaintive ugliness. Under a worn coat of paint, the thin wooden walls seemed to shiver in the wind that had risen with the end of the snowfall.

With a twitch of the left rein, Ethan checked Bay's evident intention of turning in through the broken-down gate. "The house is sort of isolated now. Before the railroad was extended through to the Flats, there was considerable traffic. I think that the railroad contributed to my mother's going downhill. When her arthritis got so bad that she couldn't move around, she would sit and watch the road. One year, while the Bettsbridge pike was being repaired after floods, Harmon Gow brought his stagecoach past here for about six months. Nearly every day, my mother would go down to the gate to see him. But after the trains started running, hardly anyone came by here. Mother couldn't understand what had happened; it weighed on her until she died."

As we turned into the Corbury road, snow began to fall again, cutting off our last glimpse of the house. Ethan returned to silence. The wind didn't cease when the snow returned. It sprang up to a gale. The landscape was tossed chaotically. But Bay was as good as Ethan's word. We pushed on, through the wild white scene, to Corbury Junction.

In the afternoon the storm held off. I finished my business as quickly as possible, and Ethan and I set out for Starkfield with a good chance of getting there for supper. But at sunset the clouds gathered again, bringing an earlier night, and the snow began to fall steadily. The snow seemed to be part of the thickening darkness. The small ray of Ethan's lantern soon was lost in a smother of falling snow. Finally, even Ethan's sense of direction and Bay's homing instinct ceased to serve us. Several times some ghostly landmark sprang up to warn us that we had gone astray and then was sucked back into the whiteness. When we finally regained our road, Bay showed signs of exhaustion. I blamed myself for having accepted Ethan's offer. I persuaded him to let me get out of the sleigh and walk through the snow at Bay's side. In this way we struggled on for another mile or two.

At last, peering into what seemed to me a formless night, Ethan said, "That's my gate yonder."

The last stretch had been the hardest. The bitter cold and the heavy going had nearly knocked the wind out of me. I could feel Bay's side ticking like a clock under my hand. "Look here, Ethan," I said. "There's no use in your going any farther."

"Nor should you," he said. "This has been enough for anyone."

I understood that he was offering me a night's shelter at his farm. I turned into the gate at his side and followed him to the barn, where I helped him to unharness and bed down tired Bay. When this was done, Ethan unhooked the lantern from the sleigh, stepped out into the night, and called to me over his shoulder: "This way."

Ethan and I headed toward a far-off square of light that trembled through the screen of snow. I staggered along behind Ethan. In the darkness I almost fell into a deep drift against the front of the house. Ethan scrambled up the porch's slippery steps, digging a path through the snow with his heavily booted foot. Then he lifted his lantern, found the latch, and led the way into the house.

I followed into a low, unlit passage with a ladder-like staircase at the back. On our right a line of light marked the door of the room that had sent its ray across the night. Behind the door a woman droned complainingly.

Ethan stamped on the worn oilcloth to shake the snow from his boots. He set his lantern on a kitchen chair that was the hall's only furniture. Then he opened the door.

"Come in," he said.

As he spoke, the droning woman fell silent.

That night I found the clue to Ethan Frome and began to put together this version of his story.

CHAPTER 2

Starkfield lay under two feet of snow, with higher drifts at windy corners. The stars shone like cold fires in an iron sky. The moon had set, but the night was so transparent that the white house-fronts between the elms looked gray against the snow, bushes looked black, and the church's basement windows sent shafts of yellow light far across the waves of snow.

Twenty-eight-year-old Ethan Frome walked quickly along the deserted street, past the bank, past Michael Eady's new brick store, and past the Varnums' house with the two black Norway spruces at its gate. Opposite the Varnums' gate, where the road fell away toward Corbury Valley, the church reared its slim white steeple.

Ethan walked toward the church. Light

from the basement windows illuminated many fresh furrows in the track leading to the basement door. A line of sleighs with heavily blanketed horses stood under an adjoining shed.

The night was still. The air was so dry and pure that it gave little sensation of cold. The atmosphere reminded Ethan of an exhausted radio receiver. Four years earlier he had taken a year's course at a technological college in Worcester, Massachusetts. He had dabbled in the laboratory with a friendly physics professor. Images supplied by that experience periodically returned at unexpected moments. His father's death, and the misfortunes following it, had put a premature end to Ethan's studies. Although they hadn't continued long enough to be of much practical use, they had fed his imagination and made him aware of large, cloudy meanings behind the daily face of things.

As Ethan strode through the snow, the sense of such meanings glowed in his brain. He paused before the church. Breathing quickly, he looked up and down the empty street. The slope of the Corbury road, below the Varnums' spruces, was Starkfield's favorite sledding ground. On clear evenings the church corner rang until late with the sledders' shouts. Tonight, however, no sled darkened the whiteness of the long slope. Midnight's hush lay on the village. All of its waking life was gathered behind the church windows, from which dance music flowed, along with the broad bands of yellow light.

Ethan went down the slope toward the basement door. To avoid being seen, he made a circuit through the untrod snow. Keeping in shadow, he edged his way to the nearest window, holding back his straight, spare body and craning his neck until he could glimpse the room.

Seen from the pure, frosty darkness in which Ethan stood, the room seemed to seethe in a mist of heat. The gas jets' metal reflectors sent waves of light against the whitewashed walls. The iron flanks of the stove at the end of the hall looked as if they were heaving with volcanic fires.

Young women and men thronged the room. A row of kitchen chairs stood against the wall facing the window. The music stopped, and older women rose from these chairs. The musicians—a fiddler and a young woman who played the harmonium on Sundays—took refreshments at one corner of a table filled with near-empty pie dishes and ice cream saucers.

The guests were preparing to leave. They moved toward the passage where coats and wraps were hung. Then Dennis Eady—a sprightly young man with thick black hair—shot into the middle of the floor and clapped his hands. The signal took instant effect. The musicians hurried back to their instruments. The dancers, some already half muffled for departure, fell into line down each side of the room. The older spectators slipped back to their chairs. After diving here and there amid the throng, Dennis drew forth a young woman who already had wound a cherry-colored scarf around her head. This woman was Mattie Silver, the cousin of Ethan's wife. Leading Mattie to the end of the floor, Dennis whirled her down its length to the bounding tune of a Virginia reel.

Ethan's heart beat fast. He had been straining for a glimpse of Mattie's dark head. Dennis danced well, and Mattie caught his fire. As she passed down the line, her light figure swinging from hand to hand in circles of increasing swiftness, the scarf flew off her head and stood out behind her shoulders. At each turn, Ethan caught sight of her laughing, panting lips; the cloud of dark hair about her forehead; and the dark eyes that seemed the only fixed points in a maze of flying lines.

The dancers went faster and faster. To keep up with them, the musicians belabored their instruments like jockeys lashing horses in the home stretch of a race. Nevertheless, it seemed to Ethan that the reel never would end. Now and then he turned his eyes from Mattie's face to that of her partner. Dennis had an impudent look of ownership. He was Michael Eady's son, as skilled at winning women's hearts as his father was at making money. Previously Ethan had found Dennis unlikable. Now he found him detestable. He thought it strange that Mattie didn't feel the same way. How could she lift her rapt face to Dennis's and drop her hands into his without seeming offended by his look and touch?

Ethan was in the habit of walking into Starkfield to fetch Mattie home on the rare evenings when a social event drew her to the village. Mattie had come to live with the Fromes to help Zeena, without pay. Because she had come from Stamford, Connecticut— a much livelier place than Starkfield—Zeena thought that Mattie should take advantage of opportunities to socialize.

When Zeena had first proposed that Mattie have an occasional evening out, Ethan had resented having to go two miles to Starkfield and back after a hard day on the farm. But he soon wished that Starkfield had social events every night.

Mattie had lived at the farm for a year. Ethan saw her frequently, from early morning until supper. But no moments in her company compared to those when they walked back, arm in arm, to the farm, her light step flying to keep up with his long stride.

Ethan had liked Mattie from the first day, when he'd driven to the train station to meet her. She had smiled and waved to him from the train, crying out, "You must be Ethan!" As she had jumped down with her bundles, he had looked over her slight build and thought, "She doesn't look like someone cut out for housework, but at least she doesn't seem to be a complainer."

The arrival in his home of hopeful young life had been like the lighting of a fire on a cold hearth. Mattie was bright and serviceable. Ethan could show and tell her things, and Mattie remembered them.

Ethan felt the sweetness of his communion with Mattie most intensely during their night walks back to the farm. He'd always been sensitive to natural beauty. Even in his unhappiest moments, field and sky aroused deep emotion in him. Previously this emotion had remained in him as a silent ache, a sadness that veiled the beauty that evoked it. He hadn't even known if anyone else felt as he did. Then he had discovered that Mattie did. He could talk to her about the constellations: "That's Orion yonder. The cluster there—like swarming bees—that's the Pleiades." Standing before a ledge of granite thrusting up through fern, he could hold Mattie entranced with talk of the Ice Age. It pleased him that she felt wonder and also admired his knowledge. Exquisite sensations drew them together with a shock of silent joy: the cold red of sunset behind winter hills, the flight of clouds over slopes of golden stubble, the intensely blue shadows of hemlocks on sunlit snow. When Mattie once said to him, "It looks like a painting," Ethan felt that someone had, at last, uttered what he felt in his soul.

As Ethan stood in the darkness outside the church, these memories returned with the poignancy of vanished things. Watching Mattie whirl down the floor from hand to hand, he wondered how he ever could have thought that his talk interested her. He was merry only in her presence, but she could be merry without him. That pained him. It seemed to indicate that she didn't need or want him. The face that she lifted to her dancing partners—a face like a window that has caught the sunset—was the same face that she showed *him*. He even noticed two gestures that he had thought she reserved for him: a way of throwing her head back when she was amused, as if to taste her laugh before she let it out, and a way of slowly sinking her eyelids when something charmed or moved her. The sight made him unhappy and roused latent fears.

Zeena never had shown any jealousy, but lately she increasingly grumbled over the housework and found indirect ways of calling attention to Mattie's inefficiency. Zeena was sickly. Ethan had to admit that she might need a stronger helper than Mattie, who had no natural gift for housekeeping. Mattie was quick to learn but didn't seem to take housework seriously. Ethan thought that if she were to marry a man she loved, her domestic instincts might awaken and her pies and biscuits become the pride of the county. As of now, though, homemaking held little interest for her.

At first Mattie had been so awkward that Ethan couldn't help laughing at her. But she had laughed back, and that had made them better friends. Ethan did his best to supplement Mattie's unskilled efforts, getting up earlier than previously to light the kitchen fire, carrying in the wood overnight, and neglecting the mill in order to help Mattie around the house. He even crept down on Saturday nights to scrub the kitchen floor after Zeena and Mattie had gone to bed. One day, Zeena had unexpectedly found him churning. She had given him a probing look and turned away silently.

Lately there had been other signs of Zeena's disfavor. One cold winter morning, as Ethan had dressed in the dark, his candle flickering in a draft from the ill-fitting window, she had said flatly from the bed behind him, "The doctor wants me to have a helper."

Ethan had turned and looked at her where she lay indistinctly outlined under the dark calico quilt. The whiteness of her pillow had given her high-boned face a grayish tinge. "A helper?" Ethan had replied.

"A hired girl. When Mattie goes."

Ethan had turned away. Taking up his razor, he had stooped to catch the reflection of his stretched cheek in the blotched mirror above the washstand. "Why would Mattie go?"

"When she gets married," Zeena had said.

"She wouldn't leave us as long as you needed her," Ethan had said, scraping at his chin.

"I wouldn't want people to say that I stood in the way of Mattie marrying a smart fellow like Dennis Eady."

Taken aback, Ethan hadn't replied.

"The doctor wants me to have a helper," Zeena had repeated. "He said I should talk to you about a girl he's heard about who might come."

Ethan had laid down the razor and straightened himself with a laugh. "Dennis Eady! If that's all you're worried about, there's no hurry to look around for a girl."

"I want to talk to you about it," Zeena had insisted.

Ethan had dressed in fumbling haste. "All right, but I don't have time now. I'm already late."

Zeena had watched him in silence as he pulled his suspenders over his shoulders and jerked his arms into his coat. She had said sharply, as Ethan went toward the door, "I guess you're always late now that you shave every morning."

That thrust had frightened him more than any insinuations about Dennis. It was true that since Mattie's arrival Ethan had taken to shaving every day. He hadn't thought about Zeena's noticing the change. In his mind, Zeena had gone from an oppressive reality to something insubstantial. His entire life was lived within sight and sound of Mattie, and he couldn't imagine his life any other way.

But now, as Ethan stood outside the church and saw Mattie spinning down the floor with Dennis, a throng of disregarded hints and threats wove a cloud around his brain.

CHAPTER 3

As the dancers poured out of the hall, Ethan drew back behind the open storm door and watched groups split up. Now and then a moving lantern ray lit a face flushed from eating and dancing. The villagers walked to Main Street while their farm-dwelling neighbors packed themselves into the sleighs under the shed.

"Aren't you riding, Mattie?" a woman called from the crowd at the shed.

Ethan's heart jumped.

Mattie answered, "No. Not on such a beautiful night." She was right inside the door. In another moment she would step out into the night, and Ethan would see her.

A wave of shyness pulled Ethan back into the dark angle of the wall. From the beginning of his relationship with Mattie, her expressiveness, ease, and freedom had made *him* more expressive and relaxed. But now he felt as awkward as in his student days, when he had periodically tried to amuse young women. He hung back.

Mattie came out alone and paused a few yards from Ethan. She looked around uncertainly.

Then Dennis approached. He came so close to Mattie that, under their formless wrappings, they seemed to merge into one dim outline. "Has your gentleman friend gone back on you?" he said half mockingly. "I won't tell anyone."

Ethan thought, "I hate his cheap banter."

"I have my father's sleigh and colt," Dennis continued.

"Why?" Mattie asked gaily.

In a tone that was half bragging, half romantic, Dennis answered, "I knew I'd want to take a ride tonight."

Mattie hesitated, twirling the end of her scarf around her fingers. With dread, Ethan awaited her answer.

Springing toward the shed, Dennis called to her, "Hold on while I unhitch the colt."

Mattie stood perfectly still, looking after him.

Dennis lead out the colt, climbed into the sleigh, and flung back the bearskin to make room for Mattie at his side.

Mattie turned and darted up the slope toward the front of the church. "Goodbye!" she called back over her shoulder. "I hope you have a lovely ride."

Dennis laughed and gave the colt a whip cut that brought him quickly abreast of Mattie's retreating figure. "Come on. Get in. It's slippery." He leaned over to reach out a hand to her.

Mattie laughed. "I'm not getting in. Good night."

By this time they had moved beyond Ethan's hearing. Ethan observed the shadowy pantomime of their silhouettes. Mattie and Dennis moved along the crest of the slope above him. After a moment, Dennis jumped from the sleigh and went toward Mattie with the reins over one arm. He tried to slip his other arm through hers, but she nimbly eluded him. Ethan's heart, which had swung out over a black void, trembled back to safety. A moment later he heard the jingle of departing sleigh bells and discerned a figure advancing alone toward the empty expanse of snow before the church.

Ethan caught up with Mattie in the black shade of the Varnums' spruces.

She turned quickly. "Oh!"

"Did you think that I'd forgotten you, Matt?" Ethan asked with bashful glee.

She answered seriously, "I thought maybe you couldn't come for me."

"What on earth could stop me?"

"Zeena wasn't feeling well today."

"She went to bed long ago." Ethan paused, struggling with a question. "You were going to walk home alone?"

Mattie laughed. "I'm not afraid."

They stood together in the gloom of the spruces. Wide and gray under the stars, an empty world glimmered around them.

Ethan forced himself to ask, "If you thought I wasn't coming, why didn't you ride back with Dennis?"

"How did you know that? Where were you?"

Ethan laughed, feeling clever. "Come along." He slipped his arm through hers and slightly pressed his arm against her side.

Neither of them moved. It was so dark under the spruces that Ethan barely could see the shape of Mattie's head beside his shoulder. He longed to stoop and rub his cheek against her scarf. He wished he could stand there with her all night.

Mattie moved forward a step and paused

above the dip of the Corbury road. Its icy slope, scored by the runners of innumerable sleds, looked like a scratched mirror. "Lots of sledders were out here before the moon set," she said.

"Would you like to sled with them some night?" Ethan asked.

"Oh Ethan, could we? That would be lovely!"

"We'll come tomorrow if there's moon-light."

Mattie lingered, pressing closer to Ethan's side. "Ned Hale and Ruth Varnum nearly crashed into the big elm at the bottom." She shivered. "Wouldn't it have been awful? They're so happy."

"Ned isn't good at steering. I can take you down safely." Ethan knew that he was bragging, but joy had unsteadied him. The tone of Mattie's "They're so happy" had suggested that she was thinking of Ethan and herself.

"The elm is dangerous, though. It should be cut down," Mattie said.

"Would you be afraid of it with me?"

She tossed back, "I told you I'm not afraid." She walked on rapidly.

Mattie's mood changes were Ethan's

despair and joy. The motions of her mind were as incalculable as a bird's flitting in the branches. He attached enormous importance to every change in her look and tone. Her dismissal of Dennis had filled him with joy. Now her abrupt manner chilled him. He mounted School House Hill at her side and walked on in silence until they reached the lane leading to the sawmill. Then his need for some assurance grew too strong. "You'd have found me right away if you hadn't gone back for that last reel with Dennis," he said awkwardly. He couldn't say the name "Dennis" without his throat muscles stiffening.

"How could I tell you were there?"

Instead of answering, Ethan blurted out, "I suppose that what people say is true."

Mattie stopped short and faced him. "What do people say?"

"That you'll leave us," he floundered on.

"Is that what they say? Zeena isn't happy with me?" Their arms had slipped apart. They stood motionless, each trying to see the other's face. "I know I'm not as capable as I should be," Mattie said. "I still do many things awkwardly, and my arms aren't very strong. But if Zeena just would tell me, I'd try. She hardly ever says anything. Sometimes I can see that she's displeased, but I don't know why."

She turned on Ethan with sudden indignation. "You should have told me, Ethan, unless you also want me to go!"

The cry was balm to his raw wound. The iron heavens seemed to melt and rain down sweetness. He struggled to express himself but could say only, "Come along."

Mattie and Ethan walked on in silence through the blackness of the hemlock-shaded lane and out again into the comparative clearness of the fields. On the farther side of the hemlock belt, the open country rolled away before them gray and lonely under the stars. Sometimes their way led them under the shade of an overhanging bank or through the thin obscurity of a clump of leafless trees. Here and there a farmhouse stood far back among the fields, as mute and cold as a gravestone. The night was so still that they heard the frozen snow crackle under their feet. The crash of a loaded branch falling far off in the woods reverberated like a gun shot. Once, a fox barked. Mattie shrank closer to Ethan and quickened her steps.

At length they sighted the group of larches at Ethan's gate. As they drew near it, Ethan said, "Then, you don't want to leave us, Matt?"

He had to stoop to hear her soft reply: "Where would I go if I did?"

The answer sent a pang through him, but the tone suffused him with joy. He forgot what else he had meant to say and pressed her against him so closely that he seemed to feel her warmth in his veins. "You aren't crying, are you, Matt?"

"Of course not," she said shakily.

They turned in at the gate and passed under the shaded knoll where, enclosed by a low fence, the Frome gravestones slanted at various angles through the snow. Ethan looked at them. For years the buried dead had mocked his restlessness, his desire for change and freedom. "We never got away. How could *you*?" seemed to be written on every headstone. Whenever he went in or out of his gate, he thought with a shiver, "I'll just go on living here until I join them." But now all desire for change had vanished. The sight of the little enclosure gave him a warm sense of continuity and stability.

"I guess we'll never let you go, Matt," Ethan said softly, as though even the dead, lovers once, must conspire with him to keep her. Brushing by the graves, he thought, "We'll always live here together, and some day she'll lie there beside me."

They climbed the hill to the house.

Halfway up the slope, Mattie stumbled against some unseen obstruction and clutched Ethan's sleeve to steady herself. A wave of warmth went through him. For the first time he stole his arm around her. She didn't resist. They walked on as if they were floating on a summer stream.

Zeena always went to bed right after supper. The house's shutterless windows were dark. A dead cucumber vine dangled from the porch like a crepe streamer tied to a door after a death. Ethan thought, "If Zeena were dead . . ." Then he pictured Zeena lying in their bedroom asleep, her mouth slightly open, her false teeth in a tumbler by the bed.

Ethan and Mattie walked around to the back of the house. It was Zeena's habit, when they came back late from Starkfield, to leave the key to the kitchen door under the mat.

Ethan stood before the door, his arm still around Mattie. "Matt," he began, not knowing what he intended to say.

Mattie slipped from his hold without speaking.

Ethan stooped down and felt for the key. "It's not there," he said, straightening himself with a start.

They strained their eyes at each other

through the icy darkness. Such a thing never had happened before.

"Maybe she forgot," Mattie said in a tremulous whisper. But they both knew that it wasn't like Zeena to forget. They stood listening intently. Then Mattie continued, "It might have fallen off into the snow."

Ethan felt in his pocket for a match. Kneeling down, he passed its light slowly over the rough edges of snow around the doorstep. He was still kneeling when his eyes, level with the door's lower panel, caught sight of a faint ray beneath it. He heard a step on the stairs. Then the door opened, and he saw Zeena.

Zeena stood tall and angular against the kitchen's dark background. With one hand, she held a quilted bedspread to her flat chest. With the other, she held a lamp. Level with her chin, the light illuminated her puckered throat and the bony wrist of the hand that clutched the quilt. The light ghoulishly deepened the hollows and prominences of her high-boned face under its ring of curlers. Ethan felt as if he never before had known what his wife looked like.

Zeena stepped aside without speaking. Mattie and Ethan passed into the kitchen, which had a vault's deadly chill.

"I guess you forgot about us, Zeena," Ethan said, stamping the snow from his boots.

"No. I just felt too sick to sleep."

Mattie came forward, unwinding her wraps. Her lips and cheeks were the same cherry color as her scarf. "I'm sorry, Zeena. Is there anything I can do?"

"No." Zeena turned from her. "You should have shaken that snow off outside," she said to Ethan. She walked out of the kitchen ahead of Mattie and Ethan. Pausing in the hall, she raised the lamp at arm's length, as if to light their way up the stairs.

Ethan hung his coat and cap on a peg. The doors of the two bedrooms faced each other across the narrow upper landing. Tonight it was especially repugnant to him that Mattie should see him follow Zeena. "I'm not coming up yet," he said, turning back toward the kitchen.

Zeena stopped short and looked at him. "For heaven's sake, what are you going to do down here?"

"I'll go over the mill accounts."

Zeena stared at him. The flame of the unshaded lamp brought out her face's fretful lines. "At this time of night? You'll catch your death of cold. The fire went out long ago."

Without answering, Ethan moved toward the kitchen. As he did so, he looked at Mattie, who sent him a warning glance. The next moment, Mattie mounted the stairs ahead of Zeena.

"I guess you're right," Ethan said. "It *is* cold down here." With lowered head, he followed Zeena up and into their room.

Ethan and Zeena didn't say a word after their bedroom door closed. Zeena measured out some drops from a medicine bottle, swallowed them, wrapped her head in a piece of yellow flannel, and lay down with her face turned away.

Ethan hurriedly undressed and blew out the light so that he wouldn't see Zeena when he took his place at her side. As he lay there, he heard Mattie moving around in her room. Her candle, sending its small ray across the landing, drew a scarcely perceptible line of light under his door. He kept his eyes fixed on the light until it vanished. Then the room grew perfectly black, and nothing was audible except Zeena's asthmatic breathing. Ethan thought of the warmth of Mattie's shoulder against his. Why hadn't he kissed her? Previously he hadn't dared to think of kissing her. Now, however, he felt that her lips rightly were his.

CHAPTER 4

The next day, Ethan was out early to haul some wood. The winter morning was as clear as crystal. The sunrise burned red in a pure sky. The shadows on the woodlot's rim were dark blue. Beyond the white, sparkling fields, patches of far-off forest hung like smoke.

In the early morning stillness, while his muscles swung to their familiar task and his lungs breathed in mountain air, Ethan pictured Mattie's face in the red of the sun and the glitter of the snow. How she had changed since her arrival in Starkfield! He remembered what a colorless little thing she was when he met her at the station. The whole first winter, she had shivered with cold when northerly gales shook the thin clapboards and snow beat like hail against the loose-hung windows. He had feared that Mattie would hate the cold, loneliness, and hard life, but she showed no discontent. According to Zeena, Mattie was bound to make the best of her situation because she had nowhere else to go. But Zeena, who continually complained, didn't apply that principle to herself.

Ethan pitied Mattie. Misfortune had forced her into unpaid servitude. Mattie was the daughter of Zeena's cousin Orin Silver. Orin had excited envy and admiration in the family by moving to Connecticut, marrying a Stamford woman, and taking over her father's thriving pharmacy. But Orin ran the business into the ground and died in debt. Mattie's mother died soon after. At twenty, Mattie was left with nothing but fifty dollars from the sale of her piano. She was unequipped to earn a living. Basically, she could trim a hat, make molasses candy, recite a poem she had learned in school, and play a few tunes on the piano. When she tried to learn stenography and bookkeeping, her health broke down. For six months she worked as a department store clerk, but standing behind a counter further weakened her.

Mattie's father had persuaded her closest relatives to entrust their savings to him, and he had used up the money. After his death, these relatives were willing to give Mattie advice but, understandably, no financial assistance. When Zeena's doctor urged Zeena to find a helper, the family thought of Mattie. Zeena doubted Mattie's abilities but liked being able to find fault with someone without much risk of losing her. So Mattie came to Starkfield.

Zeena's fault-finding was the silent kind. During the first months, Ethan alternately burned with a desire to see Mattie defy Zeena and trembled with fear of the result. Then the situation grew less strained. Pure air and long summer hours in the open gave Mattie new life. Having more time to focus on her complex ailments, Zeena grew less watchful of Mattie. Ethan, struggling under the burden of his barren farm and failing sawmill, felt that peace reigned in the house. Now, however, Ethan felt dread because of Zeena's obstinate silence and Mattie's look of warning.

Ethan didn't finish his hauling until midday. The timber was to be delivered to Andrew Hale, a Starkfield builder. Ethan loaded the logs onto a wagon, to which he hitched his two shaggy gray horses, Slate and Gray. Just as he was about to set out for Starkfield, he recalled Mattie's warning look.

"If there's going to be trouble, I want to be here," he thought. He instructed the hired man, Jotham Powell, to unhitch the horses and take them back to the barn.

Ethan and Jotham then trudged through the fields to the house. When they entered the kitchen, Mattie was lifting the coffee from the stove and Zeena was seated at the table. Ethan stopped short at the sight of her. Instead of her usual calico bathrobe and knitted shawl, she wore her best dress, of brown wool. A bonnet rose above her thin hair, tightly waved from curlers. Hand luggage and a small clothing box stood on the floor beside her.

"Where are you going, Zeena?" Ethan exclaimed.

"I have such bad shooting pains that I'm going to Bettsbridge," she said matter-of-factly. "I'll spend the night with Aunt Martha and see that new doctor."

Twice before, Zeena had suddenly gone off to Bettsbridge to seek the advice of some new doctor. Ethan dreaded these trips because of their cost. Zeena always came back loaded with expensive remedies. On her last trip she had paid twenty dollars for an electric battery that she never used. For the moment, however, Ethan's relief was so great that it precluded all other feelings. He now had no doubt that Zeena's reason for staying awake the night before was, in fact, that she'd felt unwell.

Zeena continued, "If you're too busy with the hauling, Jotham can drive me to the train."

Ethan hardly heard what she was saying. He was thinking that she wouldn't return before the following evening.

"I can't go on the way I am much longer," she complained. "The pains are all the way down to my ankles now."

"Jotham will drive you over," Ethan said. He suddenly realized that he was looking at Mattie while Zeena talked to him. With an effort he turned his eyes to his wife.

Zeena sat opposite the window. The pale light reflected from the banks of snow made her face look more drawn and bloodless than usual. It sharpened the three parallel creases between her ear and her cheek and drew peevish lines from her thin nose to the corners of her mouth. Although she was only seven years older than Ethan, she already was old.

Ethan tried to say something suitable, but there was only one thought in his mind: for the first time since Mattie had come to live with them, Zeena would be away overnight. He wondered if Mattie was thinking the same thing.

Zeena pushed her plate aside and measured out a dose from a large bottle at her elbow. "It hasn't done me any good, but I might as well use it up," she said. Pushing the empty bottle toward Mattie, she added, "If you can clean away the medicine taste, we can use the bottle for pickles."

CHAPTER 5

As soon as Zeena drove off, Ethan took his coat and cap from the peg. Mattie was washing the dishes, humming a dance tune from the previous night.

Ethan said, "So long, Matt."

Mattie answered gaily, "So long, Ethan."

The kitchen was warm and bright. Sunlight slanted through the south window onto Mattie; the cat, Purr, who was dozing in a chair; and the geraniums brought in from the doorway, where Ethan had planted them in the summer to "make a garden" for Mattie. Ethan would have liked to linger, watching Mattie tidy up and then settle down to her sewing, but he wanted even more to finish the hauling and be back home before nightfall.

All the way to Starkfield, Ethan thought about his return to Mattie. The kitchen wasn't

tidy and shining as it had been during his boy-
hood, but in Zeena's absence it had a homey
feel. He pictured what it would be like that
evening, when he and Mattie were there after
supper. For the first time they would be alone
together indoors. They would sit, one on each
side of the stove, like a married couple.
Smoking his pipe, he would sit in his socks.
Mattie would laugh and talk in her special way.

Ethan's spirits soared. Usually silent, he
whistled and sang as he drove through the
snowy fields. His troubles, and the long
Starkfield winters, hadn't completely extin-
guished his capacity for joy. Naturally grave
and inarticulate, he admired gaiety in others.
Friendly relationships warmed him to the
marrow. At Worcester, although he'd had a
reputation for being a loner, he had delighted
in being clapped on the back and greeted as
"Ethe." The end of such familiarities had
increased the chill of his return to Starkfield.

In Starkfield the silence around him had
deepened year by year. Left alone, after his
father's accident, to manage the farm and
mill, he hadn't had time to socialize. When his
mother had fallen ill, the house's loneliness
had grown more oppressive than that of the
fields. His mother had been a talker in her

day, but after her illness she rarely spoke. Sometimes, in the long winter evenings, Ethan would ask her, in desperation, why she didn't "say something." She would lift a finger and answer, "Because I'm listening."

Speech returned to the house only when Ethan's cousin, Zenobia Pierce, came from the next valley to help him nurse his mother. After so much silence, Zeena's talk was music to Ethan's ears. Zeena laughed at him for not knowing the simplest sickbed duties. She told him to "go along" and leave her to see to things. Ethan felt free to go about his business again and talk with other men. Zeena's efficiency shamed and dazzled him. He felt grateful. When his mother died, Zeena told him to hitch up and go for the undertaker. She found it strange that he hadn't decided beforehand who would have his mother's clothes and sewing machine. After the funeral, when Ethan saw Zeena preparing to go away, he was seized with a dread of being alone at the farm. Before he knew what he was doing, he asked her to stay. Since then, he often thought, "I wouldn't have married Zeena if my mother had died in spring instead of winter."

When Ethan and Zeena married, they agreed to sell the farm and sawmill and move to a large town. Ethan wanted to be an engineer and live in a town where there were lectures, libraries, and "people doing things." An engineering job in Florida, which came his way during his time in Worcester, increased his faith in his ability as well as his eagerness to see the world. He felt sure that, with a "smart" wife like Zeena, he would do well.

Zeena's native village was slightly larger and nearer to the railway than Starkfield. From the beginning of their marriage, Zeena said that she didn't want to live on an isolated farm. However, within a year—while Ethan waited, in vain, for someone to buy the farm and mill—Zeena became "sickly." When she had come to take care of Ethan's mother, she had been a model of health.

Then Zeena too fell silent. Perhaps it was the inevitable effect of life on the farm. Perhaps it was because Ethan stopped listening to her. When she spoke, it was only to complain of things that he couldn't remedy. To restrain a tendency to impatient retort, he first formed the habit of not answering her. Finally, he thought of other things while she talked. Lately, however, her silence had begun to trouble him. At times, looking at Zeena's closed face, he felt a chill of foreboding. He

recalled his mother's growing silence and
wondered if Zeena too was becoming senile.
At other times, he was even more frightened
by the thought that her silence resulted from
hidden resentments and suspicions.

When Ethan drove into Andrew Hale's
yard, the builder was getting out of his sleigh.

"Hello, Ethan!" Andrew said. "This timber will come in handy." He went up to Gray
and Slate and patted their sweating flanks.

Andrew was a ruddy man with a big gray
moustache and a stubbly double chin. His
scrupulously clean shirt always was fastened
with a small diamond stud. This display of
wealth was misleading. Although Andrew
maintained a fairly profitable business, his
careless habits and the demands of his large
family kept him in debt. He was an old friend
of Ethan's family. His house was one of the
few where Zeena occasionally visited. Zeena
was drawn there by the fact that Jane Hale,
Andrew's wife, had done more nursing than
any other woman in Starkfield and was considered an authority on symptoms and treatment.

After the logs were unloaded, Ethan
joined Andrew in the shed that served as
Andrew's office. Like Andrew, the place was
welcoming but untidy. "Sit down and thaw

out," Andrew said. Andrew sat with his feet up on the stove and his back propped against a battered desk strewn with papers. "I'm fixing up a little house for Ned and Ruth to live in when they're married," he said. "Young people like nice things. You know how it is. Not so long ago you fixed up your own place for Zeena."

After some further pleasant talk, almost exclusively by Andrew, Ethan left Slate and Gray in Andrew's stable and went about some other business in Starkfield. As he walked away, Andrew's words lingered in his ears. He reflected grimly that his seven years with Zeena seemed "not so long" to Andrew.

The afternoon was drawing to an end. Here and there a lighted pane spangled the cold, gray dusk and made the snow look whiter. The bitter weather had driven everyone indoors. Ethan had the long street to himself. Suddenly he heard the brisk play of sleigh bells. A sleigh passed him, drawn by a colt. Ethan recognized the colt as Michael Eady's. Wearing a new fur cap, Dennis Eady leaned forward and waved. "Hello, Ethan!" he shouted, and he spun on.

The sleigh was going toward the Frome farm. Ethan's heart contracted as he listened to the dwindling bells. Had Dennis heard of Zeena's departure and decided to take advantage of this chance to spend an hour with Mattie? Ethan was ashamed of his sharp jealousy, which seemed unworthy of Mattie.

Ethan walked to the church corner and entered the shade of the Varnums' spruces, where he had stood with Mattie the previous night. As he passed into their gloom, he saw an indistinct outline ahead of him. Then he recognized Ned Hale and Ruth Varnum. They kissed.

Noticing Ethan, Ruth exclaimed, "Oh!" The Varnums' gate slammed behind her while Ned hurried on ahead of Ethan.

Ethan smiled at the embarrassment he had caused. What did it matter to Ruth and Ned if they were caught kissing each other? Everybody in Starkfield knew they were engaged. It pleased Ethan to have surprised a pair of lovers on the spot where he and Mattie had stood with such a thirst for each other in their hearts. But he felt a pang at the thought that Ruth and Ned needn't hide their love.

Ethan fetched Gray and Slate from Andrew's stable and started on his long climb back to the farm. The cold was less sharp than earlier in the day. A thick, fleecy sky threatened

snow for the next day. Here and there a star
pricked through. In an hour or two the moon
would push over the ridge behind the farm,
burn a gold-edged rent in the clouds, and
then be swallowed by them. A mournful
peace hung on the fields, as though they felt
the cold's relaxing grip and stretched themselves in their long winter sleep.

Ethan's ears were alert for the jingle of
sleigh bells, but no sound broke the silence of
the lonely road. As he drew near the farm, he
saw, through the thin screen of larches at the
gate, a light twinkling in the house above
him. "She's in her room, fixing herself up for
supper," he thought. He remembered
Zeena's bitter, mocking stare when Mattie, on
the evening of her arrival, had come down to
supper with smoothed hair and a ribbon at
her neck.

Ethan passed by the graves on the knoll
and turned his head to glance at one of the
older headstones, which had deeply interested
him as a boy because it bore his name:
"Sacred to the memory of Ethan Frome and
his wife, Endurance, who dwelled together in
peace for fifty years." Previously Ethan had
thought that fifty years was a long time for
two people to live together. Now he thought
it could pass in a flash. He bitterly wondered

if a similar epitaph would mark his grave and Zeena's.

Ethan opened the barn door and looked in, half fearing that he'd see Dennis's colt in the stall beside his old orange-brown horse, Sorrel. But Sorrel was there alone, slowly chewing his food with toothless jaws. Ethan whistled cheerfully while he bedded down Slate and Gray and shook an extra measure of oats into their mangers. He sang as he locked the barn and sprang up the hill to the house.

Ethan reached the kitchen porch and turned the door handle, but the door didn't yield to his touch. Startled at finding it locked, he rattled the handle. Then he reflected that Mattie was alone. It was natural that she should lock the door at nightfall. He stood in the darkness expecting to hear her step. After vainly straining his ears, he called out, "Matt!"

A minute later he heard a sound on the stairs and saw a line of light around the door frame. He heard the key turn. The door opened, and Mattie faced him.

Mattie stood just as Zeena had stood the night before. She held a lamp in her hand, against the kitchen's black background, at the same level. With the same distinctness it highlighted her slim young throat and childishly small wrist. Then, striking upward, it threw a lustrous fleck on her lips, edged her eyes with velvet shade, and laid a milky whiteness above the dark curve of her brows.

Mattie wore her usual dark dress, and there was no bow at her neck. But she had run a crimson ribbon through her hair. This new adornment transformed and glorified her. She seemed to Ethan taller, fuller, more womanly in shape and motion. Smiling, she stood aside while he entered. She moved away from him in a soft, flowing way. She placed the lamp on the table, which was carefully set for supper. The food on the table included fresh doughnuts, stewed blueberries, and Ethan's favorite pickles in a red glass dish. A bright fire glowed in the stove. Purr lay stretched before it, watching the table with a drowsy eye.

Ethan was overcome with a sense of wellbeing. He went into the passage to hang up his coat and pull off his wet boots. When he returned, Mattie had set the teapot on the table, and Purr was rubbing against her ankles.

"Purr, I nearly tripped over you," Mattie said with a merry glint sparkling through her lashes.

Ethan felt renewed jealousy. Was Mattie's face so bright because Dennis had visited her?

"Any visitors, Matt?" he asked.

She nodded and laughed, "Yes. One."

Ethan scowled. "Who?"

Her eyes danced with pleasure. "Jotham. He came in after he got back and asked for a cup of coffee before he went home."

Relief flooded Ethan's brain. "I guess he got Zeena to the train all right."

"Yes. In plenty of time."

Zeena's name threw a chill between them. For a moment they stood looking sideways at each other. Then Mattie said with a shy laugh, "I guess it's time for supper."

They drew their seats up to the table. Purr jumped between them into Zeena's empty chair. "Purr!" Mattie said. They laughed.

Mattie sat with downcast eyelids, sipping her tea while Ethan feigned an insatiable appetite for doughnuts and sweet pickles. At last, after casting about for an effective opening, he took a long gulp of tea, cleared his throat, and said, "Looks like there'll be more snow."

Mattie feigned great interest. "Do you think so? Do you think it will interfere with Zeena's getting back?" She blushed as the question escaped her and hastily set down her cup.

Ethan reached over for another helping of pickles. "This time of year you never can tell. There can be large drifts on the Flats."

"Purr!" Mattie cried. Unnoticed, Purr had crept up from Zeena's seat to the table. He was elongating his body in the direction of the milk jug, which stood between Ethan and Mattie. The two leaned forward at the same moment, and their hands met on the jug's handle. Mattie's hand was underneath. Ethan kept his clasped on it a moment longer than was necessary. Retreating, Purr backed into the pickle dish, which fell to the floor with a crash.

Mattie sprang from her chair and kneeled by the fragments. "Oh, Ethan. It's in pieces! What will Zeena say?"

"Whatever she says will have to be said to Purr," he answered, laughing. He kneeled at Mattie's side to scrape up the swimming pickles.

Mattie lifted stricken eyes to him. "Zeena didn't want the dish to be used, not even when there was company. I had to get up on the stepladder to get it down from the top shelf of the china closet, where she keeps her best things. She'll want to know why I did that."

"She won't know anything if you don't

tell her. Tomorrow I'll get another dish just like it. Where did it come from? If I have to, I'll go to Shadd's Falls for it."

"It was a wedding present. Don't you remember? It came all the way from Philadelphia, from Zeena's aunt who married the minister. That's why she wouldn't ever use it. Oh, Ethan, what should I do?" She started to cry.

Ethan felt her tears pour over him like burning lead. "Don't, Matt."

Mattie struggled to her feet. Ethan rose and followed her helplessly. She spread out the pieces of glass on the kitchen counter. They seemed to be the shattered fragments of their evening.

In a voice of sudden authority, Ethan said, "Give them to me." Mattie drew aside, instinctively obeying. Ethan gathered the pieces of glass into his broad palm and walked out of the kitchen to the passage. He lit a candle, opened the china closet, and, reaching his long arm up to the highest shelf, laid the pieces together with such accuracy that it was impossible to detect from below that the dish was broken. If he glued it together the next morning, months might pass before Zeena noticed what had happened. Meanwhile he might be able to find the same dish in Shadd's Falls or Bettsbridge.

Ethan returned to the kitchen with a lighter step. Mattie was removing the last pickles from the floor. "It's all right, Matt. Come finish supper," Ethan said firmly. Reassured, Mattie shone on him through tear-hung lashes. Ethan's soul swelled with pride as he saw how his tone comforted her. She didn't even ask what he had done. Except when he was steering a big log down the mountain to his mill, he never had known such a thrilling sense of mastery.

CHAPTER 6

Mattie and Ethan finished supper. While Mattie cleared the table, Ethan went to look at the cows and then took a last turn around the house. The earth lay dark under a muffled sky. The air was so still that now and then he heard a lump of snow thump down from a tree far off on the edge of the woodlot.

When Ethan returned to the kitchen, Mattie had pushed his chair up to the stove and seated herself near the lamp with some sewing. The scene was just as he had dreamed of it that morning. He sat down, drew his pipe from his pocket, and stretched his feet to the glow. His hard day's work in the keen air made him feel lazy and lighthearted. He had a sense of being in another world, where all was changeless warmth and harmony. The only negative was that he couldn't see Mattie from where he sat. After a moment he said, "Come sit by the stove."

Zeena's empty rocking chair faced him. Mattie rose and sat in it. As her brown head rested against its patchwork cushion, Ethan had a momentary shock, picturing Zeena in the same chair. As if affected by a similar uneasiness, Mattie changed her position, leaning forward to bend her head over her work, so that Ethan saw only the tip of her nose. Then Mattie rose, saying, "I can't see well enough to sew," and went back to her chair by the lamp.

Ethan made a pretext of getting up to replenish the stove. When he returned to his seat, he pushed it sideways so that he could view Mattie's profile and the lamplight falling on her hands. Purr, a puzzled observer of these unusual movements, jumped up into Zeena's chair, rolled himself into a ball, and lay watching Ethan and Mattie with narrowed eyes.

Deep quiet sank on the room. The clock ticked above the mantel, now and then a piece of charred wood fell in the stove, and the geraniums' faint scent mingled with the odor of Ethan's smoke, which began to throw a blue haze around the lamp and hang grayish cobwebs in the room's shadowy corners.

All constraint vanished between Mattie

and Ethan. They began to talk easily and simply. They spoke of everyday things: the prospect of snow, the next church social, Starkfield's loves and quarrels. The commonplace nature of their conversation produced in Ethan an illusion of longstanding intimacy that no emotional outpouring could have created. He imagined that Mattie and he always had spent, and always would spend, their evenings this way.

"This is the night we were going to go sledding, Matt," Ethan said at length, with the comfortable knowledge that they could go on any other night.

Mattie smiled. "I guess you forgot."

"I didn't forget. It's pitch dark outside. We might go tomorrow if there's moonlight."

Mattie laughed with pleasure, her head tilted back. The lamplight sparkled on her lips and teeth. "That would be lovely."

Ethan kept his eyes fixed on her, marveling at the way her face changed with each turn of their talk, like a wheat field under a summer breeze. "Would you be scared to sled down the Corbury road with me on a night like this?"

Mattie's cheeks reddened. "I wouldn't be any more scared than *you* would."

"Well, I'd be scared. That's an ugly corner

down by the big elm. If a person didn't keep their eyes open, they'd go right into it." He enjoyed feeling protective and authoritative. "We're better off here."

Mattie's eyelids sank slowly, in the way that Ethan loved. "Yes, we're better off here."

Her tone was so sweet that Ethan took the pipe from his mouth and drew his chair up to the table. Leaning forward, he touched the brown material that she was hemming. "Say, Matt, what do you think I saw under the Varnums' spruces, coming home just now? I saw a friend of yours getting kissed." The words had been on his tongue all evening, but now that he'd spoken them, they struck him as vulgar and out of place.

Mattie blushed and moved her needle more rapidly. "I guess it was Ruth and Ned," she said in a low, somber voice.

Ethan had hoped that his reference to the lovers would lead to pleasant chitchat that might lead, in turn, to a harmless caress, such as touching Mattie's hand. But now he felt awkward. He remembered that the night before, when he had put his arm around Mattie, she hadn't resisted. But that had been outside, under the open sky. Now, in the warm, lamp-lit room, with its many reminders of daily routine and propriety, Mattie seemed infinitely farther away and more unapproachable. To ease his constraint, Ethan said, "I guess they'll be setting a date soon."

"Yes. I wouldn't be surprised if they were married by the summer." Mattie seemed to caress the word *married*.

A pang shot through Ethan. Twisting away from her in his chair, he said, "I guess it'll be your turn next."

Mattie gave an uncertain laugh. "Why do you keep saying that?"

Ethan echoed her laugh. "To get used to the idea, I guess."

He drew up to the table again. Mattie sewed on in silence, with dropped lashes. With fascination Ethan contemplated the way her hands went up and down above the material, just as a pair of birds fly back and forth over a nest they're building.

At length, without turning her head or lifting her eyelids, Mattie said quietly, "It's not because Zeena wants to get rid of me?"

"What do you mean?" Ethan stammered.

Mattie raised distressed eyes to his, dropping her work on the table between them. "I don't know. I thought last night that she wanted to be rid of me. She hasn't said anything to you?"

Ethan shook his head. "Not a word."

With a laugh, Mattie tossed the hair back from her forehead. "I guess I'm just nervous, then. I won't think about it anymore."

"No, let's not think about it, Matt!" The sudden heat of Ethan's tone made Mattie blush. She sat silent, her hands clasped on her work. It seemed to Ethan that a warm current flowed toward him along the material that lay unrolled between them. He cautiously slid his hand, palm downward, along the table until his fingertips touched the end of the material. A faint vibration of Mattie's lashes indicated that she was aware of his gesture and that it sent a current back to her. She let her hands lie motionless on the other end of the material.

As they sat this way, Ethan heard a sound behind him and turned his head. Purr had jumped from Zeena's chair to dart at a mouse. As a result of the sudden movement, the empty chair had set up a ghostly rocking. "Zeena will be rocking in it this time tomorrow," Ethan thought. "I've been in a dream. This is the only evening Mattie and I ever will have together." The return to reality was as painful as the return to consciousness after anesthesia.

The change in Ethan's mood spread to Mattie. She looked up at him languidly, as though her eyelids were weighted with sleep and it was an effort to raise them. Her glance fell on his hand, which still grasped the material. Ethan saw a slight tremor cross her face. Without thinking, he lowered his head and kissed the material that he held.

Mattie rose and silently rolled up her work. She fastened it with a pin and put it, along with her thimble and scissors, into a pretty box that Ethan once brought her from Bettsbridge.

Ethan also stood. He looked vaguely around the room. The clock above the mantel struck eleven.

"Is the fire all right?" Mattie asked in a low voice.

Ethan opened the stove door and poked aimlessly at the embers. When he raised himself again, he saw that Mattie was dragging Purr's bed, a box lined with carpet, toward the stove. Then Mattie recrossed the floor and moved two of the geranium pots away from the cold window. Ethan followed her and brought the other geraniums, the hyacinth bulbs in a cracked custard bowl, and the German ivy trained over an old croquet arch.

When these nightly duties were done, there was nothing left to do except bring in the tin candlestick from the passage, light the candle, and blow out the lamp. Ethan put the candlestick in Mattie's hand, and she left the kitchen ahead of him.

"Good night, Matt," Ethan said as she put her foot on the first step of the stairs.

Mattie turned and looked at him a moment. "Good night, Ethan." And she went up.

When the door of her room had closed, Ethan realized that he hadn't even touched her hand.

CHAPTER 7

The next morning at breakfast, Jotham joined Ethan and Mattie for breakfast. Ethan felt joyful. His evening with Mattie had given him a vision of what life at her side might be. He was glad that he hadn't done anything to destroy the evening's sweetness.

A last load of timber needed to be hauled to Starkfield. Jotham had come to help with the job. A wet snow, melting to sleet, had fallen during the night and turned the roads to glass. Ethan and Jotham believed that the temperature would rise by the afternoon and melt much of the dangerous ice, making travel safer. So Ethan proposed to Jotham that they load the wagon at the woodlot, as they had done the previous morning, and delay bringing the load to Starkfield until later in the day. This plan would enable Ethan to send

Jotham to the train station after dinner to meet Zeena while he himself took the lumber down to Starkfield.

Ethan told Jotham to go out and harness Gray and Slate. For a moment he and Mattie had the kitchen to themselves. She had plunged the breakfast dishes into a tin dishpan and was bending above it with her slim arms bared to the elbow. Steam from the hot water beaded her forehead and tightened her hair into little brown rings.

Ethan stood looking at her, his heart in his throat. He wanted to say, "We'll never be alone like this again." Instead he took his tobacco pouch down from a shelf, put it into his pocket, and said, "I guess I'll be home for dinner."

Mattie answered, "All right, Ethan."

Ethan heard her singing over the dishes as he went. He intended to send Jotham back to the farm as soon as the wagon was loaded. He himself would walk to Starkfield to buy glue for the pickle dish.

However, on the way to the woodlot, Slate slipped on ice and cut his knee. When Ethan and Jotham got him up again, Jotham had to go back to the barn for a rag with which to bind the cut.

Then, when the loading finally began, a sleety rain came down. The timber was so slippery with ice that it took twice as long as usual to lift the logs and get them in place on the wagon. Slate and Gray shivered and stamped under their wet blankets.

When the job was done, it was long past dinnertime. Ethan had to give up the idea of going to Starkfield. He wanted to lead Slate home and wash his cut.

As soon as dinner was over, Ethan headed back to the woodlot. Jotham still was drying his wet feet at the stove. Ethan could only give Mattie a quick look and say, "I'll be back early."

Mattie nodded.

Ethan trudged off through the rain. After he had unloaded the timber at Andrew Hale's, he hurried to Michael Eady's store for glue. Dennis was lounging by the stove with some friends. The group greeted Ethan, but no one knew where to find the glue. Ethan waited impatiently while Dennis made an ineffectual search.

"If you'll wait until my father comes, he probably can find it," Dennis said.

"I'll see if I can get some at Mrs. Homan's," Ethan said.

Dennis then boasted that Alice Homan's store wouldn't have anything that couldn't be found at Eady's.

Paying no attention, Ethan left for the rival store. After a long search, Alice found a single bottle of glue among the cough lozenges and corset laces.

"I hope Zeena hasn't broken anything she values," Alice called after Ethan as he turned Gray and Slate toward home.

The fitful bursts of sleet had changed to steady rain. Slate and Gray had heavy work even without a load behind them. Once or twice, hearing sleigh bells, Ethan turned his head, thinking that Zeena and Jotham might reach home before him, but he didn't see them. Ethan set his face against the rain and urged the horses on.

The barn was empty when Gray and Slate turned into it. After quickly tending to them, Ethan strode up to the house and pushed open the kitchen door. Mattie was there alone. She was bending over a pan on the stove. At the sound of Ethan's step, she turned with a start and sprang to him.

"Look, Matt. I've got some glue to mend the dish with."

"Zeena's back," Mattie whispered, clutching Ethan's sleeve.

They stood and stared at each other, pale as culprits.

"But Sorrel isn't in the barn," Ethan stammered.

"Jotham brought some goods from the train station for his wife. He drove right on home with them."

Ethan gazed blankly around the kitchen, which looked cold and squalid in the rainy winter twilight. "How's Zeena?" he whispered.

"I don't know. She went right up to her room."

"She didn't say anything?"

"No."

Ethan thrust the bottle of glue back into his pocket. "Don't worry. I'll come down during the night and mend the dish." He pulled on his wet coat again and returned to the barn to feed Slate and Gray.

While he was there, Jotham drove up with Sorrel and the sleigh.

When the horses had been fed, Ethan said to Jotham, "You might as well come to the house for a bite." He wanted Jotham's neutralizing presence at the supper table. Zeena always was especially irritable after a trip.

Although seldom unwilling to accept a free meal, Jotham opened his stiff jaws and slowly answered, "Thank you, but I'll go along back."

Ethan was surprised. "You'd better come and dry off. Supper will be something nice and hot."

Jotham simply repeated, "I'll go along back."

To Ethan there was something ominous in Jotham's rejection of free food and warmth. Had Zeena complained so much to Jotham that he was eager to leave?

When Ethan re-entered the kitchen, the lamp illuminated the same scene of shining comfort as on the previous evening. The table had been as carefully laid, a clear fire glowed in the stove, Purr dozed in its warmth, and Mattie came forward carrying a plate of doughnuts.

She and Ethan looked at each other in silence. Then she said, as she had said the night before, "I guess it's time for supper."

CHAPTER 8

Ethan went out into the passage to hang up his wet garments. He listened for Zeena's step and, not hearing it, called her name up the stairs. She didn't answer.

After a moment's hesitation, Ethan went up and opened Zeena's door. The room was almost dark, but he saw Zeena sitting by the window, bolt upright. She still was in her traveling dress.

"Well, Zeena," Ethan ventured from the threshold. She didn't move. "Supper's almost ready. Aren't you coming down?"

"I couldn't touch a morsel," she replied.

"I guess you're tired after the long ride."

Turning her head, Zeena answered solemnly, "I'm much sicker than you think."

She'd said this many times before. Ethan wondered if this time it finally was true. He stepped into the dim room. "I hope that isn't so, Zeena."

She continued to gaze at him through the twilight and said, in a self-important tone, "I've got complications." Almost everyone in the neighborhood had specific "troubles," but only a select few had "complications." People struggled on for years with "troubles," but "complications" nearly always meant death.

Ethan alternately felt hope that Zeena *was* dying and pity for her. She looked hard but lonely, sitting there in the darkness. "Is that what the new doctor told you?"

"Yes. He says I need an operation."

Ethan was alarmed by the possible expense. "No one ever told you that before. What do you know about this doctor?"

Annoyed, Zeena said, "I didn't need to have anyone tell me that I've been losing ground every day. Everyone but you could see that. And everyone in Bettsbridge knows about Dr. Buck. His main office is in Worcester. Every two weeks, he comes to Shadd's Falls and Bettsbridge for consultations. Eliza Spears was wasting away with kidney trouble before she went to him. Now she's up and around and singing in the choir."

"I'm glad to hear that. You must do as Dr. Buck advises," Ethan answered sympathetically.

Zeena still was looking at him. "I intend to."

Ethan was struck by a new note in her voice. It was neither whining nor reproachful, but dryly resolute. "What does he advise?" he asked, with a mounting vision of expenses.

"He wants me to have a hired girl. He says I shouldn't do any housework."

"A hired girl?" Ethan stood transfixed.

"Yes. Aunt Martha already found me one. Everyone said I was lucky to get a girl to come out here. I agreed to give her a dollar extra to make sure that she'd come. She'll be here tomorrow afternoon."

Ethan felt anger and dismay. He had foreseen an immediate demand for money but not a permanent drain on his scant resources. He no longer believed that Zeena's condition was serious. He saw her trip to Bettsbridge as a plot hatched by her and her relatives. "If you intended to hire a girl, you should have told me beforehand," Ethan said angrily.

"How could I tell you beforehand? How did I know what Dr. Buck would say?"

Ethan gave a short laugh of disbelief. "Oh, yes. Dr. Buck. Did he tell you how I'm to pay the girl's wages?"

Zeena was furious. "No, he didn't. I'd have been ashamed to tell him that you begrudge me the money needed to restore my health, even though I lost my health nursing your mother!"

"You lost your health nursing my mother?"

"Yes. And my relatives said at the time that you couldn't do any less than marry me after all my effort."

"Zeena!"

Their words darted at each other like serpents shooting venom. Suddenly Ethan felt horrified and ashamed at fighting this way. He turned to the shelf above the chimney, groped for matches, and lit the one candle in the room. At first its weak flame didn't reduce the shadows. Then Zeena's face stood out grimly against the uncurtained windowpane, which had turned from gray to black. It was the first scene of open anger between the couple in their sad seven years together.

"You know I don't have the money for a hired girl. You'll have to send her back."

"Dr. Buck says it'll be my death if I go on slaving the way I have. He doesn't understand how I've survived *this* long."

"Slaving!" Ethan restrained himself. "You won't have to lift a hand. I'll do everything around the house myself."

"You already neglect the farm." Then

Zeena added sarcastically, "You'd better send me to the poorhouse and be done with it. I guess Fromes have been there before."

The taunt burned into Ethan, but he let it pass. "I haven't got the money. It can't be helped. You're a poor man's wife, but I'll do the best I can for you."

For a while Zeena sat motionless, her arms stretched along the arms of her chair, her eyes fixed on emptiness. "I guess we'll make out," she said mildly.

The change in her tone reassured Ethan. "Of course we will. I can do more for you, and Mattie..."

Zeena interrupted. "We won't be housing and feeding Mattie anymore."

"Won't be housing...?"

Zeena laughed in a way he never had heard before. "Did you think I was going to keep two girls? No wonder you were scared at the expense."

Ethan felt confused. He couldn't register the idea of Mattie's departure. "I don't know what you mean. Mattie isn't a hired girl. She's your relative."

"She's a pauper who's hung onto us after her father did his best to ruin my kin. She's been here a whole year. Let someone else take her in now."

There was a tap on the closed door. "Ethan! Zeena!" Mattie said cheerfully from the other side of the door. "It's late. Supper has been ready half an hour."

After a moment, Zeena called out from her seat, "I'm not coming down."

"Oh! You aren't well enough? Should I bring you something?"

Ethan roused himself with an effort and opened the door. "Go back down, Matt. Zeena's just tired. I'm coming."

"All right," Mattie answered. She quickly went back downstairs.

Ethan shut the door again and turned back into the room. Zeena's face was unchanged. He felt helpless. "Are you really going to send Mattie away?"

"I never intended for her to stay here the rest of her life."

Ethan became vehement. "You can't throw her out. She has no money or friends. She's done her best for you, and she has nowhere to go. You might forget that she's your kin, but other people won't. What do you think people will say about you?"

Zeena waited a moment, as if giving Ethan time to feel the full force of the contrast between his agitation and her composure.

Then she replied in the same smooth voice, "I know well enough what they say about my having kept her here as long as I have."

Ethan's hand dropped from the doorknob, which he had gripped since he closed the door. His wife's retort was like a knife-cut across his sinews. He had intended to plead, to argue that it didn't cost much to keep Mattie and that he could fix up the attic for a hired girl. But Zeena's words made him feel powerless. "You're going to tell her to leave right away?"

As if trying to make Ethan see reason, Zeena said, "The new girl will be here tomorrow. She has to have somewhere to sleep."

Ethan looked at Zeena with loathing. She no longer was the sullen, listless, self-absorbed creature who had lived at his side. Now she was an evil force. There never had been anything in her that someone could appeal to. Now she had mastered him. Mattie was her relative, not his. He couldn't force Zeena to keep Mattie under her roof. His entire miserable past—his youth of failure, his recent hardship and vain effort—rose up bitterly in his soul and took the shape of Zeena, who had barred his way at every turn. She had taken everything else from him. Now she intended to take the one thing that could make up for everything else. Ethan clenched his fist in hatred. He stepped toward Zeena but then stopped. Calming himself, he said, "You're not coming down, then?"

"No. I'll lay down for a while," she answered mildly.

Ethan turned and walked out of the room.

In the kitchen Mattie was sitting by the stove, with Purr curled up on her knees. She sprang to her feet as Ethan entered and carried the covered dish of meat pie to the table. "Is Zeena sick?" she asked.

"No."

Mattie shone at him across the table. "Well, sit down. You must be starving." She uncovered the meat pie and pushed it over to him. Her eyes were happy.

Ethan began to eat mechanically. Then disgust overwhelmed him, and he laid down his fork.

Mattie was looking at him tenderly. "What's the matter, Ethan? Doesn't it taste right?"

"It's first-rate. I just . . ." He pushed his plate away, rose from his chair, and walked around the table to Mattie's side.

Mattie started up with frightened eyes. "There's something wrong!" She seemed to melt against him in her terror. Ethan caught her in his arms, held her fast, and felt her lashes beat against his cheek like netted butterflies. "What is it?" she stammered.

At last, Ethan kissed her. He was unconscious of everything except the joy that this gave him.

Mattie lingered a moment, caught in the same strong current. Then she slipped from him and drew back a step, pale and troubled. Her look smote him with regret.

As if he saw her drowning, Ethan cried out, "You can't go, Matt! I won't let you!"

"Go? Must I go?" she stammered.

Ethan was ashamed that he had lost control and flung the news at her so brutally. His head reeled. He leaned against the table for support.

"Ethan, what's happened? Is Zeena mad at me?"

Mattie's questions steadied him, although they deepened his anger and pity. "No, it's not that. This new doctor has scared her. He's told her she won't get well unless she doesn't do any housework."

Mattie stood silent, drooping like a broken branch. She was so small and weak-looking that it wrung Ethan's heart. Suddenly she lifted her head and looked straight at him.

"She wants someone better than me at house-work. Is that it?"

"She wants to hire a girl."

After a long silence, Mattie quietly said, "Don't be sad, Ethan."

"Oh, God," he groaned. The glow of passion he had felt for her had melted to an aching tenderness. He saw her eyelids beating back tears. He longed to take her in his arms and soothe her.

"Your supper's getting cold," Mattie said with a weak attempt at cheerfulness.

"Oh, Matt. Matt. Where will you go?"

Her eyelids sank, and a tremor crossed her face. For the first time she clearly envisioned her future. "I might get a job in Stamford," she said without genuine hope.

Ethan dropped back into his seat and hid his face in his hands. Despair seized him at the thought of her setting out alone to look for work. No one would help her. What were her chances of finding a decent job? She was untrained and inexperienced. He sprang up. "You can't go, Matt! I won't let you. Zeena always has had her way. Now I intend to have mine."

Mattie quickly lifted her hand as a warning gesture. Ethan heard Zeena approaching. With her usual dragging step, Zeena entered the room and quietly took her usual seat between Mattie and Ethan. "I feel a bit better," she said. "Dr. Buck says I should eat all that I can to keep up my strength, even if I don't have any appetite." She reached across Mattie for the teapot. She had changed from her good wool dress to her usual calico bathrobe and knitted brown shawl. She also wore her usual face and manner. She poured out her tea, added lots of milk to it, helped herself to meat pie and pickles, and, as usual, adjusted her false teeth before she began to eat. Purr rubbed against her. She said, "Good boy," stooped to stroke him, and gave him a scrap of meat from her plate.

Ethan sat speechless, not eating. Mattie nibbled at her food and asked Zeena a few questions about her visit to Bettsbridge. Zeena answered in her everyday tone and, warming to the subject, vividly described some of her friends' and relatives' intestinal ailments. She looked straight at Mattie as she spoke, a faint smile deepening the vertical lines between her nose and chin.

When supper was over, Zeena rose from her seat and pressed her hand to her flat chest. "Your meat pie always is a little heavy, Mattie," she said without meanness. "I think I'll find the stomach powders that I got last year in

Springfield. I haven't used them for a while. Maybe they'll help with this heartburn."

Mattie lifted her eyes. "Shall I get them for you, Zeena?"

"No. They're in a place you don't know about." Zeena left the kitchen.

Mattie began to clear the dishes from the table. As she passed Ethan's chair, their eyes met and clung together desolately. The warm, still kitchen looked as peaceful as the previous night. Purr had sprung into Zeena's rocking chair, and the fire's heat was beginning to draw out the geraniums' scent.

Ethan dragged himself to his feet. "I'll go out and take a look around," he said, going toward the passage to get his lantern.

As Ethan reached the door, he met Zeena re-entering the room. Her lips were twitching with anger. Her yellowish face was flushed with excitement. The shawl had slipped from her shoulders and was dragging at her down-trodden heels. In her hands she carried the fragments of the red glass pickle dish. "I'd like to know who did this," she said, looking sternly from Ethan to Mattie.

There was no answer.

Zeena continued in a trembling voice, "I went to get the powders I'd put in my father's old eyeglass case, on the top shelf of the china closet, where I keep the things I value, so that people won't meddle with them, and..." Her voice broke. Two small tears hung on her lashless eyelids and slowly ran down her cheeks. "You can't reach the top shelf without a stepladder. When we were married, I put Aunt Philura's pickle dish up there on purpose. It's never been down since, except during spring cleaning, and then I always lifted it with my own hands, so that it wouldn't break." She laid the fragments reverently on the table. "I want to know who did this," she said with a trembling voice.

"Purr did it," Ethan said.

"Purr?"

"That's what I said," Ethan said defiantly.

Zeena looked at him hard and then turned her eyes to Mattie, who was carrying the dishpan to the table. "I'd like to know how Purr got into my china closet."

"Chasing mice, I guess," Ethan said. "There was a mouse around the kitchen all last evening."

Zeena continued to look from Ethan to Mattie. Then she gave her small, strange laugh. "I knew Purr was a smart cat, but I didn't know he was smart enough to pick up the pieces of my pickle dish and lay them edge to edge on the very shelf he knocked them off."

Mattie drew her arms out of the steaming water. "It wasn't Ethan's fault, Zeena. Purr did break the dish, but I took it down from the china closet."

Zeena stood beside her ruined treasure, stiffening into stony resentment. "You took my pickle dish down? What for?"

Mattie blushed. "I wanted to make the supper table pretty."

"You wanted to make the supper table pretty. And you waited until my back was turned and took the thing I value most and wouldn't ever use, even when the minister came to dinner or Aunt Martha came from Bettsbridge." Zeena gasped as she considered the full extent of this treachery. "You're a bad girl, Mattie Silver. I've always known it. Your father was the same way. I was warned of it when I took you in. I tried to keep my things where you couldn't get at them, and now you've taken from me the thing I valued most." After a short spasm of sobs, Zeena returned to stone. "If I'd listened to people, you'd have gone before now, and this wouldn't have happened." Tenderly, mournfully gathering up the bits of broken glass, she left the room and went up to bed.

CHAPTER 9

Ethan and Mattie stood speechless. Then Mattie returned to clearing up the kitchen for the night. Ethan took his lantern and went on his usual round outside the house.

When Ethan returned to the kitchen, it was empty. His tobacco pouch and pipe had been laid on the table. Under them was a note written on a scrap of paper torn from the back of a seed catalogue: "Don't worry, Ethan."

When Ethan had been called back to the farm by his father's illness, his mother had given him a small room behind the parlor for his own use. He had nailed up bookshelves there, built a sofa out of boards and a mattress, laid out his papers on a kitchen table, hung an engraving of Abraham Lincoln and a calendar with "Thoughts from the Poets" on the rough plaster wall, and tried to produce some likeness to the study of a minister who had been kind to him and lent him books while he was at Worcester. Ethan took refuge in this room during the summer. But when Mattie had come to the farm, he had given her the room's stove, so the room was uninhabitable during cold months.

As soon as the house was quiet, Ethan descended to this retreat. Entering the cold, dark "study," he placed the lantern on the table and, stooping to its light, read the message again and again. It was the first time that Mattie ever had written to him. Possessing the paper gave him a sense of her nearness. It also deepened his anguish by reminding him that soon they would have no other way of communicating with each other. Cold paper and dead words would replace her lively smile and warm voice.

Rebellion stirred within Ethan. He was too young, strong, and full of life to easily submit to the destruction of his hopes. Must he wear out all his years at the side of a bitter, complaining woman? He had sacrificed numerous possibilities to Zeena's narrow-mindedness and ignorance. What good had come of it? She was a hundred times more bitter and unhappy than when he had married her. She took pleasure in hurting him.

He wrapped himself in his old raccoon

coat and lay down on the sofa to think. Under his cheek he felt a hard object with strange protuberances. It was a cushion that Zeena had made for him when they were engaged— the only piece of needlework he'd ever seen her create. He flung it across the floor and propped his head against the wall.

Ethan knew of a man over the mountain— a man about his own age—who had escaped from a life of misery by going west with the woman he loved. His wife had divorced him, and he had married his beloved and prospered. Ethan had seen the couple the previous summer at Shadd's Falls, where they were visiting relatives. They had a little girl, with fair curls, who wore a gold locket and was dressed like a princess. The deserted wife hadn't done badly either. Her husband had given her the farm, and she had managed to sell it. With that money and the alimony that she received, she had opened a Bettsbridge restaurant that was very successful. Ethan was fired by the thought of leaving with Mattie the next day. He would hide his hand luggage under the seat of the sleigh; Zeena wouldn't suspect anything until she went upstairs for her afternoon nap and found a letter on the bed.

Ethan sprang up, re-lit the lantern, and sat down at the table. He rummaged in the drawer for a sheet of paper, found one, and began to write: "Zeena, I've done all I could for you, and it hasn't been any use. I don't blame you, and I don't blame myself. Both of us probably will do better separately. I'm going west. You can sell the farm and mill and keep the money."

His pen paused on the word "money," which reminded him of his circumstances. If he gave the farm and mill to Zeena, what would he have left? Out west he'd be able to find work, but would he earn enough to support Mattie as well? And what about Zeena? The farm and mill were mortgaged to the limit of their value. Even if she found a purchaser—which was unlikely—it was doubtful that she'd make even a thousand dollars on the sale. Meanwhile, how would she keep the farm going? It was only by ceaseless labor and personal supervision that Ethan drew a meager living from his land. Even if Zeena were in better health than she imagined, she never could bear such a burden alone. Well, she could go back to her relatives, and seek their assistance. She was forcing that fate on Mattie. By the time she discovered his whereabouts and filed for divorce, he'd probably be earning enough to pay her sufficient alimony. The alternative was to let Mattie leave alone.

Ethan had scattered the contents of the table drawer in his search for a sheet of paper. As he took up his pen, his eye fell on an old copy of the *Bettsbridge Eagle* and this advertisement: "Trips to the West: Reduced Rates." He drew the lantern nearer and eagerly scanned the fares. Then the paper fell from his hand, and he pushed aside his unfinished letter. He realized that he didn't even have enough money to go west with Mattie. The facts closed in on him like prison wardens handcuffing a convict.

He crept back to the sofa, stretching himself out with limbs so leaden that he felt they never would move again. Tears rose in his throat and slowly burned their way to his eyelids. As he lay there, moonlight began to filter through the windowpane. Rising on his elbow, he watched the landscape whiten. This was the night on which he and Mattie had planned to go sledding, and there was the moonlight to light their way. He looked out at the slopes bathed in luster. The night's beauty seemed to mock his wretchedness.

Ethan fell asleep. When he awoke, the chill of the winter dawn was in the room. He felt cold, stiff, and hungry. He rubbed his eyes and went to the window. A red sun stood over the gray rim of the fields, behind trees that looked black and brittle. He thought, "This is Matt's last day here." As he stood there, he heard a step behind him.

Mattie entered. "Oh, Ethan. Were you here all night?" She looked small and pinched, in her poor dress, with her red scarf wound around her and the cold light turning her paleness yellowish. "You must be frozen," she said, fixing lusterless eyes on him.

He drew a step nearer. "How did you know I was here?"

"I heard you go downstairs after I went to bed. I listened all night, and you didn't come up."

He looked at her tenderly and said, "I'll make up the kitchen fire."

They went to the kitchen. Ethan fetched the coal and kindling and cleared out the stove for Mattie while she brought in the milk and the leftovers of meat pie. When the stove began to radiate warmth and the first ray of sunlight lay on the kitchen floor, Ethan's dark thoughts melted in the mellower air. The sight of Mattie going about her work as he'd seen her do on so many mornings made it seem impossible that she ever would cease to be a part of the scene. He told himself that he had exaggerated the significance of Zeena's threats and that Zeena would be more reasonable with the return of daylight.

Ethan went up to Mattie as she bent above the stove. He laid his hand on her arm. "I don't want you to worry either," he said, looking down into her eyes.

She blushed warmly and whispered, "No, Ethan. I won't worry."

"Things will straighten out," he added. "Has she said anything this morning?"

"No. I haven't seen her yet."

Ethan went out to the cow barn. Jotham was walking up the hill through the morning mist. The familiar sight added to Ethan's growing sense of security.

As the two men were clearing out the stalls, Jotham rested on his pitchfork and said, "Daniel Byrne is going to the train station today at noon. He can take Mattie's trunk, so Sorrel will have an easier time when I take Mattie over in the sleigh."

Ethan looked at him blankly.

"Mrs. Frome said the new girl will be at the train station at five. I'm to take Mattie so that she can catch the six o'clock train for Stamford."

Ethan felt the blood drumming in his temples. It was a moment before he could speak. "It isn't definite that Mattie will be leaving."

"Really?" Jotham said indifferently.

They went on with their work. When they returned to the kitchen, Mattie and Zeena were at breakfast.

Zeena was unusually alert and active. She drank two cups of coffee and fed Purr the scraps left in the meat pie dish. Then she rose from her seat and, walking over to the window, snipped three yellow leaves from the geraniums. "Aunt Martha's geraniums don't have a single faded leaf. Geranium leaves fade when they aren't cared for." Then she turned to Jotham and asked, "What time did you say Daniel will be here?"

Jotham threw a hesitating glance at Ethan. "Around noon."

Zeena turned to Mattie. "Your trunk is too heavy for the sleigh. Daniel Byrne will take it to the train station."

"Thank you," Mattie said.

"I'd like to go over things with you first," Zeena said in a casual voice. "A towel is missing. And a match case."

She went out, followed by Mattie.

When the men were alone, Jotham said, "I guess I'd better let Daniel come, then."

Ethan finished his usual morning tasks around the house and barn. Then he said to Jotham, "I'm going to Starkfield. Tell Mattie not to wait for me for dinner."

Ethan felt rebellious again. He was humiliated by the part he was forced to play in Mattie's departure and by the thought of what Mattie must think of him. Conflicting impulses struggled in him as he strode to Starkfield. He had decided to do something, but he didn't know what.

The early mist had vanished. The fields lay like a silver shield under the sun. It was one of those days when winter's glitter shines through a pale haze of spring. Every yard of the road was alive with Mattie's presence. There was hardly a branch against the sky or a tangle of brambles on the bank that didn't hold some bright memory. Once, the call of a bird in a mountain ash was so like Mattie's laughter that Ethan's heart tightened.

Suddenly it occurred to Ethan that Andrew Hale, who was kindhearted, might advance him fifty dollars toward payment for the delivered timber if Ethan told him that Zeena's illness made it necessary to hire a helper. The more Ethan considered this plan, the more hopeful it seemed. With fifty dollars in his pocket, nothing could keep him from being with Mattie.

Ethan's first goal was to reach Starkfield before Andrew had left for work. He knew that Andrew had a carpentry job down the Corbury road and was likely to leave his house early. Ethan's long strides grew more rapid. As he reached the foot of School House Hill, he caught sight of Andrew's sleigh in the distance. He hurried forward to meet it, but as it drew nearer, he saw that it was driven by Andrew's youngest son and that the person at his side, looking like a large upright cocoon in eyeglasses, was Jane Hale. Ethan signaled to them to stop. Jane leaned forward, her pink wrinkles twinkling with benevolence.

"Is Andrew still at home?" Ethan asked.

"Why, yes," Jane answered. "He isn't going to work this morning. He woke up with back pain. I made him put on one of Dr. Kidder's plasters and sit near the fire." Beaming maternally on Ethan, she bent over to add, "I just heard from Andrew that Zeena went to Bettsbridge to see that new doctor. I'm sorry she's feeling so bad again. I don't know anyone around here who's had more sickness than Zeena. As I always tell Andrew, I don't know what Zeena would have done without you to look after her. I used to say the same thing about your mother. You've had a hard time, Ethan." She gave him a last nod of sympathy while her son clucked to the horse.

As they drove off, Ethan stood in the middle of the road and stared after the retreating sleigh. It was a long time since anyone other than Mattie had spoken to him as kindly as Jane. Most people were either indifferent to his troubles or disposed to think it natural that a young man of his age should have carried the burden of three crippled lives. But Jane had said, "You've had a hard time, Ethan." He felt less alone with his misery. If the Hales were sorry for him, surely Andrew would respond to his appeal.

Ethan started down the road toward the Hales' house. After a few yards, he pulled up sharply, red-faced. In light of the words he'd just heard, he realized for the first time what he was about to do. He was planning to take advantage of the Hales' sympathy to obtain money under false pretences. He now saw his life as it really was. He was a poor man, the husband of a sickly woman. His desertion would leave her alone and destitute. Even if he'd had the heart to desert her, he could have done so only by deceiving kindly people who had pitied him.

He turned and slowly walked back to the farm.

CHAPTER 10

Outside the kitchen Daniel Byrne sat in his sleigh behind a big-boned gray horse who pawed the snow and swung his long head restlessly from side to side.

Ethan went into the kitchen and found Zeena by the stove. Her head was wrapped in her shawl. She was reading the book *Kidney Troubles and Their Cure*. Zeena didn't move or look up when he entered.

After a moment Ethan asked, "Where's Mattie?"

Without lifting her eyes from the page, Zeena replied, "I guess she's getting her trunk down."

The blood rushed to Ethan's face. "Getting her trunk down alone?"

"Jotham's in the woodlot, and Daniel says he can't leave his horse."

Ethan left the kitchen and sprang up the stairs. The door of Mattie's room was shut. He hesitated a moment on the landing. "Matt," he said softly. There was no answer. He put his hand on the doorknob.

Ethan had been in Mattie's room only once, in early summer, when he'd gone there to plaster a leak in the eaves. But he remembered how everything had looked: the red-and-white quilt on her narrow bed; the pretty pin cushion on the chest of drawers; over the chest of drawers, the enlarged photograph of her mother. Now these and all other tokens of Mattie's presence had vanished. The room looked as bare and comfortless as when Zeena had shown Mattie into it on the day of her arrival. Mattie's trunk stood in the middle of the floor. She sat on the trunk in her Sunday dress, her back turned to the door and her face in her hands. She hadn't heard Ethan's call because she was sobbing, and she didn't hear his step until he stood close behind her and laid his hands on her shoulders.

"Don't, Matt," Ethan urged.

Mattie started up, lifting her wet face to his. "I thought I'd never see you again."

He took her in his arms, pressing her close. With a trembling hand, he smoothed away the hair from her forehead. Mattie clung to him. He laid his lips on her hair, which was soft yet springy, like certain mosses on warm slopes. It had the faint woody fragrance of fresh sawdust in the sun.

Through the door they heard Zeena's voice calling out from below: "Daniel says you'd better hurry if you want him to take your trunk."

Mattie and Ethan drew apart with stricken faces. Mattie found her handkerchief and dried her eyes. Then, bending down, she took hold of one handle of the trunk.

"Let go, Matt," Ethan ordered.

She answered, "It takes two people to get it around the corner."

Ethan grasped the other handle, and together they maneuvered the heavy trunk out to the landing.

"Now let go," he said. He shouldered the trunk and carried it down the stairs and across the passage to the kitchen.

Zeena, who had returned to her seat by the stove, didn't lift her head from her book as Ethan passed. Mattie followed him out the door and helped him lift the trunk into the back of the sleigh. When it was in place, Ethan and Mattie stood side by side on the doorstep, watching Daniel plunge off behind his fidgety horse.

Ethan felt that his heart was bound with cords that tightened with every tick of the clock. Twice he opened his lips to speak to Mattie and found no breath. At length, as she turned to re-enter the house, he laid a detaining hand on her. "I'm going to drive you, Matt."

Mattie murmured, "Zeena wants me to go with Jotham."

"I'm going to drive you," Ethan repeated.

Mattie went into the kitchen without answering.

At dinner Ethan couldn't eat. If he lifted his eyes, they rested on Zeena's pinched face, and the corners of her straight lips seemed to quiver into a smile. She ate well, declaring that the mild weather made her feel better, and pressed a second helping of beans on Jotham, whose wants she generally ignored.

When the meal was over, Mattie went about her usual task of clearing the table and washing the dishes. After feeding Purr, Zeena returned to her rocking chair by the stove.

Jotham pushed back his chair and moved toward the door. On the threshold he turned back to Ethan. "What time should I come for Mattie?"

Ethan was standing near the window, mechanically filling his pipe while he watched

Mattie move to and fro. "You needn't come. I'm going to drive her."

Mattie blushed.

Zeena quickly lifted her head. "I want you to stay here this afternoon, Ethan. Jotham can drive Mattie over."

Mattie flung an imploring glance at Ethan, who repeated curtly, "I'm going to drive her."

Zeena said in an even tone, "I want you to stay and fix that stove in Mattie's room before the girl gets here. It hasn't worked right for nearly a month now."

Ethan's voice rose indignantly. "If it was good enough for Mattie, it's good enough for a hired girl."

"The girl who's coming told me she's used to a house with a furnace," Zeena persisted with the same mildness.

"She should have stayed there, then," Ethan flung back at her. Turning to Mattie, he said, "Be ready by three, Matt. I've got business at Corbury."

Jotham had started for the barn. Ethan strode down after him aflame with anger. His temples throbbed, and his eyes fogged. He led Sorrel out and backed him between the sleigh's shafts. As he passed the bridle over

Sorrel's head and wound the traces around the shafts, he remembered the day when he'd made the same preparations in order to drive over and meet Mattie at the train station. It was little more than a year ago, on just such a soft afternoon with a feeling of spring in the air. Sorrel looked at Ethan and, as he had that day, nuzzled the palm of Ethan's hand. One by one, all the days since then rose up and stood before Ethan.

Ethan flung the bearskin into the sleigh, climbed to the seat, and drove up to the house. When he entered the kitchen, it was empty. Mattie's bag and shawl lay by the door. He went to the foot of the stairs and listened. No sound reached him from above. Presently he thought he heard someone moving around in his deserted study. Pushing the door open, he saw Mattie, in her hat and jacket, standing with her back to him near the table.

She started at his approach. Turning quickly, she asked, "Is it time?"

"What are you doing here, Matt?" Ethan asked.

Mattie looked at him timidly and said with a wavering smile, "I was just looking around."

They returned to the kitchen without

speaking. Ethan picked up Mattie's bag and shawl. "Where's Zeena?" he asked.

"She went upstairs right after dinner. She said she had those shooting pains again and didn't want to be disturbed."

"Did she say goodbye to you?"

"No."

Looking slowly around the kitchen, Ethan said to himself with a shudder that in a few hours he would be returning to it alone. He couldn't bring himself to believe that Mattie stood there for the last time. "Come on," Ethan said, opening the door and putting Mattie's bag into the sleigh. He sprang to his seat and bent over to tuck the rug around Mattie as she slipped into the place at his side. "Go along," he said with a shake of the reins that sent Sorrel jogging placidly down the hill.

"We've got lots of time for a good ride, Matt," Ethan said, seeking her hand beneath the fur and pressing it in his. At the gate, instead of making for Starkfield, he turned Sorrel to the right, up the Bettsbridge road.

After a moment Mattie said, "Are you going around by Shadow Pond?"

Ethan laughed and answered, "I knew you'd know."

Mattie drew closer under the bearskin. Looking sideways around his coat sleeve, Ethan could just see the tip of her nose and a blown brown wave of hair. They drove slowly up the road between fields glistening under the pale sun and then bent to the right down a lane edged with spruces and larches. The lane passed into pine woods with tree trunks reddening in the afternoon sun and delicate blue shadows on the snow. As Mattie and Ethan entered the woods, the breeze fell; a warm stillness seemed to drop from the branches with the dropping pine needles. The tiny tracks of forest animals had left lace-like patterns in the snow. Pine cones dotted the snow like bronze ornaments.

Ethan drove on in silence until they reached a part of the woods where the pines were more widely spaced. Then he drew up and helped Mattie out of the sleigh. They passed between the aromatic trunks, the snow breaking crisply under their feet, until they came to a small sheet of water with steep wooded sides. From the farther bank, a single hill rising against the western sun threw a long, conical shadow across the lake's frozen surface. It was a secluded spot, full of the same silent melancholy that Ethan felt. He looked up and down the little pebbly beach until his eye lit on a fallen tree trunk half sub-merged in snow.

"That's where we sat at the church picnic last summer," Ethan reminded Mattie. The picnic had been one of the few social events they'd taken part in together. Mattie had begged Ethan to go with her, but he'd refused. Then, toward sunset, coming down from the mountain where he'd been felling timber, he'd been caught by some stray revel-ers and drawn into the merry group by the lake. Mattie, encircled by playful youths and bright as a blackberry under her wide-rim hat, had been brewing coffee over a fire. Ethan remembered the shyness he felt at approach-ing her in his coarse clothes and how her face lit up and she broke through the group to come to him with a cup in her hand. They had sat for a few minutes on the fallen log by the pond. Mattie had lost her gold locket and asked the young men to look for it. Ethan had spotted it in the moss. All of their times together seemed to be such flashes, when they suddenly came upon happiness as if they'd spotted a butterfly in the winter woods.

"That's where I found your locket," Ethan said, pushing his foot into a blueberry bush.

"I never saw anyone with sharper eyes," Mattie said. She sat down on the tree trunk, in the sun.

Ethan sat down beside her. "You were as pretty as a picture in that pink hat."

Mattie laughed with pleasure. "I guess it was the hat."

Never before had they acknowledged their mutual attraction to this extent. For a moment, Ethan had the illusion that he was a free man, wooing the woman he intended to marry. He looked at Mattie's hair and longed to touch it again and to tell her that it smelled of the woods.

Mattie rose to her feet and said, "We mustn't stay here any longer."

Ethan gazed at her vaguely, only half roused from his dream. "There's plenty of time."

They stood looking at each other as if they were straining to absorb and hold each other's image. Ethan turned and silently followed Mattie to the sleigh. As they drove away, the sun sank behind the hill and the tree trunks turned from red to gray.

Mattie and Ethan wound back to the Starkfield road. The light was still clear under the open sky.

"Matt, what will you do?" Ethan asked.

After some time, Mattie said, "I'll try to get a job in a store."

"You shouldn't do that. Last time, the bad air and constant standing damaged your health."

"I'm a lot stronger now."

"If you work in a store, you won't stay strong."

They drove for a while without speaking. Every yard of the way, some spot where they'd stood together, laughing or silent, clutched at Ethan.

"Won't any of your relatives help you?" Ethan asked.

"I wouldn't ask any of them," Mattie said.

Ethan said softly, "There's nothing I wouldn't do for you if I could."

"I know."

Ethan felt a slight tremor in Mattie's shoulder. "Oh, Matt," he broke out, "I'd go with you if I could."

Mattie turned to him, pulling a scrap of paper from her breast. "Ethan, I found this." It was the letter to Zeena that Ethan had started to write the previous night and had forgotten to destroy.

"Matt!" Ethan cried. "If I could have done it, would you have gone with me?"

"Oh, Ethan, what's the use?" Mattie tore the letter into shreds and sent them fluttering into the snow.

"Tell me, Matt! Tell me!"

After a moment, she said very softly, "I used to think of it sometimes, summer nights, when the moon was so bright that I couldn't sleep."

Ethan's heart reeled with joy. "As long ago as that?"

"The first time was at Shadow Pond."

"Was that why you gave me coffee before the others?"

"I don't know. Did I? I was very upset when you wouldn't go to the picnic with me. Then, when I saw you coming down the road, I thought maybe you'd gone home that way on purpose, and that made me glad."

They were silent again. They had reached the point where the road dipped to the hollow by Ethan's mill. As they descended, darkness descended with them, dropping down like a black veil from the heavy hemlock boughs.

"I'm tied hand and foot, Matt. There isn't a thing I can do."

"You must write to me sometimes."

"What good will writing do? I want to put

my hand out and touch you. I want to do things for you and care for you. I want to be there when you're sick and when you're lonesome."

"I'll be all right."

"You won't need me, you mean? I suppose you'll marry."

"Oh, Ethan!" Mattie cried.

"I'd almost rather have you dead than married to someone else!"

"I wish I *were* dead," she sobbed.

The sound of her weeping shook Ethan out of his dark anger. He felt ashamed. "Let's not talk this way."

"Why shouldn't we, when it's true? I've been wishing for it every minute of the day."

"Matt!"

"You're the only person who's ever been good to me."

"Don't say that, when I can't lift a finger to help you."

"It's still true."

They had reached the top of School House Hill. Starkfield lay below them in the twilight. A sleigh, mounting the road from the village, passed by in a joyous flutter of bells. Ethan and Mattie straightened themselves and looked ahead with rigid faces.

Along Main Street, lights had begun to shine from house fronts. Stray figures were turning in here and there at the gates. With a touch of his whip, Ethan roused Sorrel to a languid trot.

As Mattie and Ethan approached the end of Starkfield, children's cries reached them. They saw a group of boys, with sleds behind them, scattering across the open space before the church.

"I guess this will be their last sledding for a day or two," Ethan said, looking up at the mild sky.

Mattie was silent.

"We were going to go sledding last night. We never went down together except that one time last winter," Ethan said.

"I rarely got to Starkfield," Mattie said.

They had reached the crest of the Corbury road. Between the church and the spruces, the slope stretched away below them with no sled in sight. On impulse Ethan said, "How would you like me to take you down now?"

Mattie forced a laugh. "There isn't time."

"There's all the time we want. Come on!" His one desire was to postpone the moment of turning Sorrel toward the train station.

"The girl will be waiting at the station," Mattie said.

"Let her wait. You'd have to wait if she didn't. Come on!"

Ethan jumped from the sleigh. Somewhat reluctantly, Mattie let him help her out. "There isn't any sled around," she said.

"Yes, there is. Right there under the spruces." Ethan threw the bearskin over Sorrel, who stood passively by the roadside, hanging his head. Ethan caught Mattie's hand and drew her after him toward the sled. Mattie seated herself, and Ethan took his place behind her, so close that her hair brushed his face.

"All right, Matt?" Ethan called out.

Mattie turned her head. "It's awfully dark. Are you sure you can see?"

Ethan laughed. "I could go down this hill with my eyes closed." He sat still a moment, straining his eyes down the long hill. It was the most confusing hour of the evening, the hour when the sky merges with the land in a blur that disguises landmarks and falsifies distances. "Now!" he cried. The sled started with a bound, and they flew through the dusk, gathering smoothness and speed as they went. The hollow night opened out below them. The air sang like an organ.

Mattie sat perfectly still, but as they reached the bend at the foot of the hill, where the big elm thrust out a deadly elbow, she shrank a little closer. "Don't be scared, Matt!" Ethan cried exultantly as they spun safely past the elm and flew down the second slope.

When they reached the level ground beyond, and the speed of the sled began to slacken, Mattie gave a little laugh. They sprang off and started to walk back up the hill. Ethan dragged the sled with one hand and passed the other through Mattie's arm.

"Were you afraid I'd run you into the elm?" he asked with a boyish laugh.

"I'm never scared with you."

His joy brought on a rare fit of boastfulness. "It's a tricky place. The least swerve, and we'd never come up again. I can measure distance to a hair's breadth. Always could."

"I always say you have the sharpest eyes."

Deep silence had fallen with the starless dusk. Ethan and Mattie leaned on each other without speaking. At every step of their climb, Ethan said to himself, "This is the last time we'll walk together."

They mounted slowly to the top of the hill. When they were abreast of the church,

Ethan stooped his head to Mattie to ask, "Are you tired?"

Breathing quickly, Mattie said, "It was wonderful."

With a pressure of his arm, Ethan guided Mattie toward the Norway spruces. "This sled must be Ned's. I'll leave it where I found it." He drew the sled up to the Varnums' gate and rested it against the fence. As he raised himself, he suddenly felt Mattie close to him among the shadows.

"Is this where Ned and Ruth kissed each other?" she whispered breathlessly, flinging her arms around Ethan. Her lips, groping for his, swept over his face.

Ethan held Mattie fast in a rapture of surprise.

"Goodbye," she stammered, kissing him again.

"Oh, Matt, I can't let you go!"

She freed herself from his hold and sobbed. "I can't go either!"

"What should we do?"

They clung to each other's hands like children. Mattie's body shook with desperate sobs. Through the stillness they heard the church clock strike five.

"Oh, Ethan, it's time!"

He drew her back to him. "Time for what? I'm not going to leave you."

"If I miss my train, where will I go?"

"Where will you go if you catch it?"

Mattie stood silent, her hands lying cold and relaxed in Ethan's.

"What's the good of either of us going anywhere without the other?" he said.

Mattie remained motionless, as if she hadn't heard him. Then she snatched her hands from his, threw her arms around his neck, and pressed a drenched cheek against his face. "Ethan, take me down again!"

"Down where?"

"The hill," she panted. "Take us right off it, so that we never come up again."

"What do you mean?"

Mattie put her lips close against Ethan's ear. "Right into the big elm, so we'll never have to leave each other. You said you could do it. I'd rather die than leave you."

"Matt," Ethan groaned.

Mattie tightened her hold around his neck. Her face lay close to his. "Ethan, where will I go if I leave you? I don't know how to get along alone. You said so yourself just now. No one but you ever was good to me. And there'll be that strange girl in the house, and she'll sleep in my bed, where I used to lie awake nights and listen to hear you come up the stairs."

The words were like fragments torn from Ethan's heart. With them came the hated vision of the house he would return to: the stairs that he would go up every night, the woman who would wait for him there. The sweetness of Mattie's avowal, the wonder of knowing at last that she felt as he did, made the thought of being without her more intolerable.

Mattie pleaded between short sobs, but Ethan no longer heard what she was saying. Her hat had slipped back, and he was stroking her hair. He found her mouth again, and they seemed to be by the pond together in the burning August sun. His cheek touched hers. It was cold and full of weeping. He saw the road to the train station under the night sky and heard the train's whistle up the line.

The spruces wrapped Mattie and Ethan in blackness and silence. Ethan told himself, "Maybe death feels like this. Maybe it doesn't feel like anything at all."

Sorrel whinnied across the road. Ethan thought, "He's wondering why he hasn't been fed."

"Come," Mattie whispered, tugging at Ethan's hand.

Ethan pulled the sled out. The slope below was deserted. Everyone in Starkfield was at supper. No one crossed the open space before the church. The sky, swollen with the clouds that announce a thaw, hung as low as before a summer storm. Ethan strained his eyes through the dimness; they seemed less sharp than usual. He took his seat on the sled. Mattie instantly placed herself in front of him. Her hat had fallen into the snow; Ethan's lips were in her hair. Ethan stretched out his legs, drove his heels into the road to keep the sled from slipping forward, and bent Mattie's head back between his hands.

Suddenly Ethan sprang up again. "Get up," he said.

Mattie cowered in her seat, vehemently repeating, "No. No. No."

"Get up."

"Why?" Mattie asked.

"I want to sit in front," Ethan said.

"How can you steer in front?"

"I don't have to. We'll follow the track." Ethan dragged Mattie to her feet. "I want to feel you holding me."

His last comment seemed to satisfy her.

Ethan bent down, feeling in the obscurity for the glassy track worn by previous sledders. He placed the runners between its edges. Mattie waited while he seated himself with crossed legs in the front of the sled. Then she crouched down at his back and clasped her arms around him. Her breath on his neck made him shudder. He almost sprang from his seat. But in a flash he remembered the alternative. She was right: this was better than parting. He leaned back and drew her mouth to his.

Just as they started, Sorrel whinnied again. The familiar wistful call accompanied Mattie and Ethan down the first slope. There was a sudden drop halfway down, then a rise, and after that another long descent. Ethan felt as if they were flying far up into the cloudy night, with Starkfield far below them, falling away like a speck in space. Then the big elm shot up ahead, lying in wait at the road's bend. Between his teeth, Ethan said, "We can hit it. I know we can."

As they flew toward the tree, Mattie pressed her arms tighter. Her blood seemed to be in Ethan's veins. Once or twice the sled swerved a little under them. Ethan slanted his body to keep it headed for the elm, repeating to himself again and again, "We can hit it." The tree loomed bigger and closer. As they bore down on it, Ethan thought, "It's waiting for us. It seems to know." The sled bore down on the black projecting mass. There was a last instant when the air shot past like millions of fiery wires. Then the elm...

Looking straight up, Ethan saw a single star. Feeling enormously tired, he closed his heavy eyelids and thought that he would sleep. He heard a little animal twittering somewhere nearby under the snow. She made a small, frightened cheep like a field mouse. Ethan wondered if she was hurt. Then he understood that she must be in pain: pain so excruciating that he seemed, mysteriously, to feel it shooting through his own body. He tried in vain to roll over in the direction of the sound. He stretched his left arm out across the snow. Now he seemed to feel rather than hear the twittering. It seemed to be under his palm, which rested on something soft. The thought of the animal's suffering was intolerable to him. He struggled to raise himself. He couldn't. He continued to feel around cautiously with his left hand, thinking he might get hold of the little creature and help her. All at once he knew that the soft thing he had touched was Mattie's hair and that his hand was on her face.

Ethan dragged himself to his knees. His hand went over and over Mattie's face. The twittering came from her lips. Ethan brought his face down close to hers, with his ear to her mouth. She opened her eyes and said his name.

"Oh, Matt," he moaned.

CHAPTER 11

The complaining drone ceased as I entered Ethan's kitchen. I couldn't tell which of the two women sitting there had been the speaker.

One of them raised her tall, bony figure from her seat, not as if to welcome me—she threw me no more than a brief glance of surprise—but simply to set about preparing the meal that Ethan's absence had delayed. A slovenly calico bathrobe hung from her shoulders. The wisps of her thin, gray hair were drawn away from a high forehead and fastened at the back with a broken comb. She had pale, expressionless eyes. Her narrow lips were the same yellowish color as her face.

The other woman was much smaller and slighter. She sat huddled in an armchair near the stove. When I entered, she quickly turned her head toward me, with no corresponding movement of her body. Her hair was as gray as her companion's. Her face was as bloodless and shriveled but amber-tinted, with swarthy shadows sharpening the nose and hollowing the temples. Under her shapeless dress, her body was limp and immobile. Her dark eyes had the bright stare that spinal disease sometimes gives.

The kitchen was shabby, even for that part of the country. With the exception of the dark-eyed woman's chair, which looked like a soiled relic of luxury bought at a country auction, the furniture was of the roughest kind. Three coarse china plates and a broken-nosed milk jug had been set on a greasy table scored with knife cuts. A couple of straw-bottomed chairs and a kitchen cabinet of unpainted pine stood against the plaster walls.

"It's cold here. The fire must be almost out," Ethan said, glancing around apologetically as he followed me in.

The tall woman, who had moved away from us toward the cabinet, took no notice.

From her cushioned niche, the other woman said in a high, thin voice, "Zeena only just started the fire. She fell asleep and slept a long time. I thought I'd freeze before I could wake her and get her to attend to it."

I knew then that this was the woman who had been speaking when we entered.

Her companion, who was returning to the table with the remains of a cold mince pie in a battered pie dish, set down the unappetizing food without appearing to hear the accusation against her.

Ethan stood hesitantly before her as she advanced. Then he looked at me and said, "This is my wife. After an interval he turned toward the figure in the armchair and said, "And this is Mattie Silver."

CHAPTER 12

The next morning Ruth Hale showed great relief when I returned. She had pictured me lost in the Flats and buried under a snowdrift. She and her mother were amazed that Ethan's old horse had taken me to and from Corbury Junction through the worst blizzard of the winter. Their surprise was still greater when they heard that Ethan had taken me in for the night.

I sensed that they wanted to know my impressions of the Frome household. I decided that the best way to break down their reserve would be to meet their curiosity with reserve of my own. I therefore confined myself to saying that I had been received with kindness and that Ethan had made a bed for me in a ground-floor room that seemed to have been fitted up, in better days, as a kind of study.

"Well," Ruth said, "in such a storm I guess he felt he had to take you in. I think you're the only stranger who has set foot in that house for over twenty years. Ethan doesn't like even his oldest friends to go there, and I don't think any *do*, except for the doctor and me."

"You still go there?" I asked.

"After the accident, when I was first married, I used to go a lot. But after a while I decided it made Ethan and Mattie feel worse to see me. Then I had my own troubles. I usually drive out there around New Year's and once in the summer. I always try to pick a day when Ethan's off somewhere. It's bad enough to see Zeena and Mattie sitting there. But to see his face, when he looks around that bare place, is more than I can bear. I can remember how the place looked in his mother's day, before their troubles." By this time, Nancy Varnum had gone up to bed. Ruth and I were sitting alone, after supper, in the parlor. Ruth glanced at me tentatively, as if she'd wanted, for years, for someone else to see what she had seen at the Frome house.

"Yes, it's pretty bad, seeing the three of them there," I said.

Ruth drew her mild brows into a frown of pain. "It was awful from the beginning. I was here in the house when Mattie and Ethan were carried up. They laid Mattie in the room you're in. She and I were great friends. I wanted her to be my bridesmaid. When she came to, I went up to her and stayed all night. They gave her medicine to quiet her, and she didn't know much until morning. Then all of a sudden she woke up just like herself, looked straight at me with her big eyes, and said... Oh, I don't know why I'm telling you this." She broke off, crying.

Ruth took off her eyeglasses, wiped the tears from them, and put them on again with an unsteady hand. "Everyone heard the next day that Zeena had sent Mattie off in a hurry because she had a hired girl coming. People never could figure out why Mattie and Ethan were sledding that night, when they should have been on their way to the station to catch the train. To this day, I don't know what Zeena thought. Nobody knows Zeena's thoughts. Anyway, when Zeena heard about the accident, she immediately came and stayed with Ethan at the minister's, where they'd carried him. As soon as the doctors said that Mattie could be moved, Zeena sent for her and took her back to the farm."

"She's been there ever since?" I asked.

"Yes. There was nowhere else for her to go. Zeena has cared for her, and for Ethan, as well as she could. Considering how sick Zeena always had been, it was amazing how she cared for Mattie and Ethan. Not that she's ever given up treating her own ailments. She's continued to have sick spells. But she's had the strength to take care of Ethan and Mattie for over twenty years. Before the accident, she thought she couldn't even take care of herself." Ruth paused a moment.

"It's horrible for all of them," I murmured.

"Yes. And none of them are easy to get along with. Before the accident Mattie was. I never knew a sweeter nature. But she's suffered too much. That's what I always say when people tell me that she's soured. Zeena always was cranky, although the way she puts up with Mattie is wonderful. I've seen that myself. But sometimes the two of them get going at each other. Then Ethan's face would break your heart. When I see that, I think he's the one who suffers most. Anyway, it isn't Zeena; she's too busy." Ruth sighed. "It's a pity that they're all shut up in that one kitchen. On pleasant summer days, they move Mattie into the parlor or out into the yard, and that makes it easier. But in the winter they have to stay by the one fire that they keep going in the kitchen."

Ruth drew a deep breath, as though her memory was eased of its long burden and she had no more to say. But suddenly an impulse of complete openness seized her. She took off her eyeglasses again, leaned toward me across the beadwork table cover, and said, "At first after the accident, they all thought Mattie would die. I think it's a pity that she didn't. I said that to our minister once. He was shocked. Well, he wasn't with me that morning when she first came to. If Mattie had died, Ethan might have lived. The way they are now, there isn't much difference between the Fromes up at the farm and the Fromes down in the graveyard."

AFTERWORD

ABOUT THE AUTHOR

In wealth, social status, education, and accomplishments, Edith Wharton was the opposite of her fictional character Ethan Frome. She was born in Manhattan in 1862 to wealthy, aristocratic parents: Lucretia and George Jones. Unlike Ethan, Edith never endured poverty, had to engage in physical labor, or lacked artistic, intellectual, and social stimulation. Throughout her life, she lived in an upper-class world.

Except for brief periods in Worcester, Massachusetts and in Florida, Ethan spends his entire life in one small area of rural Massachusetts. In contrast, Edith traveled widely. When she was four, her family moved to Europe. They spent a year in Rome, traveled around Spain, resided in Paris for two years, spent some months in Germany, and then lived in Florence for two years. When Edith was ten, the family returned to their fashionable Manhattan house, but they continued to make frequent trips to Europe. In adulthood, too, Edith often visited Europe. For more than ten years, Edith lived in rural Massachusetts, in a lakeside house built to her specifications. However, in 1909 she set up permanent residence in Paris.

As a child, Edith was privately educated by tutors and governesses. She also had access to her father's large personal library. From her youth on, her study of art, languages, and literature was extensive. As an adult, she socialized with brilliant artists and intellectuals. In 1923 she became the first woman to receive an honorary doctorate from Yale University. In contrast, Ethan remains largely uncultivated and uneducated. His post-secondary education is limited to one year at a small technological college.

Again in contrast to Ethan, Edith was remarkably productive and successful. When she was thirteen, a magazine published her translations of several German poems. At fourteen, she completed her first book of original poems. At fifteen, she finished writing a short novel. Over the course of her life, she wrote more than forty books. Her writing varied widely in subject and type. Along with fiction and poetry, she wrote autobiography, literary criticism, a book on interior design, and newspaper articles on World War I. She is best known for her numerous novels, including *The House of Mirth* (1905), which brought her fame; the highly popular and acclaimed *Ethan Frome* (1911); and *The Age of Innocence* (1920), which won a Pulitzer Prize for fiction—the first ever awarded to a woman.

Whereas Ethan struggles to provide for the members of his own household, Edith was able to provide aid to numerous people. During World War I, she was actively involved in assistance to war refugees. In honor of her humanitarian work, in 1916 the French government awarded her membership in the Legion of Honor. Edith also helped establish seamstress workrooms for needy, unemployed women. Each woman received wages, free lunches, and free medical care.

Outwardly, then, Edith radically differed from Ethan. However, like him she suffered from loneliness. Ethan has no siblings and becomes an orphan in his twenties. Edith had two brothers, but they were so much older (eleven and sixteen when she was born) that she grew up feeling like an only child. Her beloved father died when she was twenty, and her mother was cold and disapproving.

Edith had no lasting sexual relationship. At twenty-three, she married Edward Wharton, a wealthy, socially prominent Boston banker twelve years her senior. Although the marriage lasted twenty-eight years before ending in divorce, Edith felt little or no sexual attraction to her husband. Edward had scant interest in art or ideas. Also, he was afflicted with increasingly severe mental illness. In a letter, Edith called marriage "misery." At age forty-six, still married to Edward, Edith fell passionately in love with journalist Morton Fullerton. She thought that she had found her soul mate. But Fullerton turned out to be sexually promiscuous, and Edith was tormented by jealousy. Their love affair ended after a few years. In parallel to Edith, Ethan marries someone who is older, mentally unwell, and largely unappreciative of beauty and knowledge. He, too, feels no sexual desire for his spouse, falls in love with someone else while still married, and experiences the joy of mutual passion only briefly.

Overall, however, Edith's life was incomparably more fulfilling than Ethan's. When Edith died of a stroke in 1937, at the age of seventy-five, she was world-renowned. Artistically, intellectually, and socially, her life had been exceptionally rich.

ABOUT THE BOOK

"To remain alive," Edith Wharton wrote in her autobiography, we mustn't allow our trail in life to become a rut. *Ethan Frome* (1911), which many critics regard as Wharton's finest novel, shows people who fail to "remain alive." The book equates life with love and intellectual growth.

When Mattie Silver first arrives at the Fromes' farm, she seems "colorless" and regularly shivers with cold. But after she and Ethan fall in love, she radiates light, warmth, and bright color. Her face "lights up" when she sees Ethan; she "shines" on him. Her eyes, lips, and teeth sparkle; her lips and cheeks are rosy. She wears a crimson hair ribbon, pink hat in summer, and cherry-red scarf in winter.

Love also enlivens Ethan. When he touches Mattie, he feels "a wave of warmth." He thinks of her as having lit a fire on a previously cold hearth. If she left and he could communicate with her only by letter, "cold paper and dead words would replace her lively smile and warm voice." To Ethan, Mattie represents "hopeful young life." He feels fully alive only in her presence.

Ethan's wife, Zeena, is the primary obstacle to Ethan and Mattie's love. Zeena is Mattie's opposite: drab, stony, and cold. Whereas Mattie's presence warms Ethan, Zeena's chills him. Because she is both unloving and unloved, Zeena is largely dead. Although she is only in her thirties, she is "old" in appearance and behavior. She lies in bed during the day and sometimes sits in the dark. Her face is "bloodless" and grayish; her lips are yellowish; her eyes are pale.

Partly because their love is thwarted, Mattie and Ethan become like Zeena. When Mattie is in her forties, her once-rosy face is "bloodless" and "shriveled"; her hair is gray. People describe the middle-aged Ethan as "stiff," "old," and "dead": "frozen" in grief.

Along with the possibility of romantic love, Ethan, Zeena, and Mattie lose the possibility of moving out into the world and growing intellectually. Their trail in life becomes a rut.

Ethan's year away at a Worcester college constitutes movement toward a wider social circle and new knowledge. At school, friendly relationships "warm" him, but he loses these relationships when he returns to Starkfield. He also loses the reading opportunities available at Worcester, where a kindly minister lent him books. Starkfield doesn't even have a library. Ethan briefly dreams of going west with Mattie, but he doesn't have enough money.

By middle age, Ethan rarely reads anything other than a nearby town's newspaper. When the narrator accidentally leaves an issue of *Popular Science* in Ethan's sleigh, Ethan reads it and is dismayed by his own ignorance. As a student, he enjoyed one brief engineering job in Florida. He wanted to be an engineer, live in a town with libraries and lectures, and "see the world." Instead he spends his days laboring at his farm and mill. Ethan has been in Starkfield "too many winters," one character says. "Most of the smart ones get away." When Ethan looks at the headstones in his family graveyard, he imagines the dead mocking his frustrated wish for freedom and change: "We never got away. How could *you?*"

Zeena never travels farther than the rural area of Massachusetts in which she was born. When she marries Ethan, they plan to move to a large town. Like Ethan, Zeena doesn't want to live on an "isolated farm." But Ethan doesn't manage to sell the farm. Within a year Zeena deteriorates from healthy to sickly.

Love for Ethan and fear of hardship prevent Mattie from leaving Starkfield and returning to Stamford, Connecticut or going elsewhere. "I'd rather die than leave you," she tells Ethan. "Where will I go if I leave you? I don't know how to get along alone." Choosing death over life, Mattie and Ethan attempt double suicide, and Mattie ends up permanently paralyzed. From then on, she is cut off from nearly all people and activities; she never again moves beyond Ethan's farm.

At the end of the book, Ruth Hale comments that it would have been better if Mattie had died in the attempted suicide. She also says that there isn't much difference between Ethan or Zeena and already-dead Fromes. Mattie, Ethan, and Zeena don't genuinely live because they never experience lasting love or sustained intellectual growth. In addition to being a tragedy, *Ethan Frome* is a powerful warning to us all.